I ESCAPED THE KILLER BEES

I ESCAPED
BOOK 14

SD BROWN

SCOTT PETERS

D1598464

I Escaped The Killer Bees (I Escaped Book Fourteen)

ISBN: 978-1-951019-41-9 (Hardcover)

ISBN: 978-1-951019-40-2 (Paperback)

Cover design by Susan Wyshynski

Best Day Books For Young Readers

I ESCAPED THE KILLER BEES

CHAPTER 1

Marana, Arizona
September 2021

Thirteen-year-old Carlos Mendoza tried to open the front door, but the knob didn't turn. He wrenched it again and realized it was locked. Fear trickled down his neck like a stream of Mama's jalapeño honey.

"Mario," Carlos said, trying to sound calm. He didn't want to frighten his little brother who was only nine and had a broken leg. "No more jokes. Toss me the house keys. Now."

"I don't have the keys," Mario said, not taking his eyes from his Spiderman comic. "They're inside."

"You locked the door?" Carlos tried not to sound upset—or as scared as he felt. It would only make things worse.

Mario shrugged. "Leave me alone. I'm reading."

Carlos whipped his gaze back toward the bee cloud hovering over the rake at the side of the house. Sweat streaked his face. He'd been digging up a clump of bunchgrass when he'd disturbed a hidden hive of underground bees.

Mouth slack, he sucked in air and watched the growing swarm rise from the ground. They had to get into the house before the bees found them. For some strange reason, the bees hadn't followed him… not yet, anyway. Had they identified the rake as the enemy? That wouldn't last long.

He started to hyperventilate.

The insect cloud grew twice its size in seconds. There had to be hundreds of bees. And more were coming out of the ground. What if these bees were Africanized killer bees like the ones in the Channel 4 news that morning?

He had to get his brother to safety.

"Come on, Mario. Put your book down. We have company," Carlos said, pointing to the swarm.

Mario's eyes went wide and his comic book slipped to the ground. "What are we going to do?"

Carlos whispered, "We have to find another way inside before they notice us."

"What if we don't?" Mario's voice squeaked.

"We will," Carlos said it like he had a plan when he had none. Shoot. Mama had left Carlos in charge, and he didn't know what to do.

Think Fast!

"Cover your head with your shirt. Follow me."

Carlos tiptoed to the kitchen window and tried to push it open. But like the door, it was locked.

"Carlos! The bee cloud is moving." Mario sounded scared. "It's by the giant saguaro cactus next to the driveway. "And headed this way."

That left one option. Not a great one. But the best one Carlos could come up with. "Run for it. Go."

"I can't," Mario whimpered. "My leg." He turned to face the swarm, raising his crutch like a baseball bat. "I'll swat 'em."

"Forget that." Carlos grabbed the crutch, threw it down, slung Mario over his shoulder, and ran for the garden shed.

"Hurry!" Mario screeched. "The swarm looks like a giant fastball. It's coming straight at us."

"Shut up," Carlos panted. Mario was heavier than he looked. "You're making things worse."

Mario's grasp tightened and Carlos's foot twisted. He almost fell. Pain raced up his shorter leg but he kept going. He had to get Mario to safety. They were almost there. Just another six feet to go. Five. Four. Three. Two.

They'd reached the shed.

He dropped Mario onto his feet and yanked open the door.

The blood pumping through his heart had given him super strength—too much. He ripped the door right off its hinges.

"Why'd you do that?" Mario said.

"I didn't mean to."

A sharp stabbing sensation pierced his neck. No. The first bee had reached them. Without looking, he knew the rest of the swarm was close behind.

Time was running out.

The sting throbbed a million times worse than any sting he'd ever had. And it wasn't his imagination. These weren't regular bees. These were killer bees!

"Quick. Drop flat on the ground," Carlos ordered. "And keep your face covered."

"We're going to die," Mario cried. "They'll swarm us and sting us all over. And we'll die."

Carlos shoved Mario down. "Just do what I tell you. Lay flat. Don't move. I've got a plan."

CHAPTER 2

2 1/2 HOURS EARLIER

Carlos sat at the kitchen table wolfing down a serious pile of pancakes slathered in butter, whipped cream, honey, and topped with a dust storm of cinnamon-sugar.

Today was Wednesday and the Marana School District had scheduled a district In-Service Day. No school. No teachers. No books.

His mom had the day off, and Carlos had plans—no watching Mario, his nine-year-old brother. Carlos was headed to the BMX Ranch.

"Slow down, mijo," his mother said, flipping another batch of pancakes on the small electric grill. "Eat too fast and you'll be sick. You can't win races that way."

"I can't be late, Mama. All the guys will be there."

"Well they won't be impressed if you lose your breakfast on the track. Now go wake your brother. He's slept long enough."

Carlos shoved half a pancake into his mouth and mumbled, "The BMX Ranch is already open for practice. Coach is running time checks to decide who races in what divisions on Saturday."

"Don't talk with your mouth full." Mama shook the spatula at him. "Wake your brother. Now. Or you will go nowhere today."

"Okay. Okay." He noisily slid his chair across the cracked tile floor. "I'm going."

Carlos limped toward the small bedroom he shared with his little brother. Mario perched on the edge of his bed in his Spiderman pajamas. Feet dangling. Swinging his broken leg with its blue strap-on cast. His thick wavy hair was in bed-head mode. He was messing with Carlos's cell phone.

"Hey." Carlos grabbed his phone.

"Please?" Mario said. "Just let me use it. For a little while?"

"What? And let you flush my phone like you did yours? I don't think so."

"Mama said we're brothers and should share." Mario grabbed for the phone.

Carlos stepped back and shoved it into his back pocket. "What Mama said is for you to get up. Or you won't get breakfast."

"Mama!" Mario shouted. "Carlos bumped my leg. He hurt it."

"He's fine," Carlos called out just in case she heard and then lowered his voice. "Don't be a brat."

He rushed into the living room, flipped on the television, and turned it up loud enough to drown out Mario if he started again. A commercial for tortilla chips blared. "Get your CRUNCH on."

"What's that?" Mama called. "I can't hear you over the television.

"Nothing," Carlos shouted.

He plopped on the couch and checked his text messages. Last time his little brother "borrowed" his phone he'd sent a bunch of stupid texts to Carlos's friends. Not cool.

Usually, Mario wasn't such a pain. But ever since he'd broken his leg, he thought he deserved special treatment. He'd slid into home plate at a Little League tournament. Now he acted like he was a hero for scoring the winning point—sacrificing his leg for the team.

Carlos glanced at the row of his brother's baseball trophies running across the top shelf of the bookcase. There was enough to open a store. He frowned. It wasn't fair he'd been born with one shorter leg than the other. Then he'd have a row of trophies instead of just the one—BMX Hot Shot Rider. "I guess one's better than none," he muttered.

"News 4 Tucson," the TV blared.

Mario hobbled in from the bedroom with one crutch and flipped down the TV's volume. With his strap-on cast, his limp matched his brother's. "No wonder your old friends think you're a loser. Only old guys watch the news."

"It's not my fault you broke your leg," Carlos shot back. "Or my fault your friends are too busy texting each other to remember you exist." As soon as the words slipped out, Carlos regretted them. Mario was just a kid and he was extra grumpy because of his broken leg. "Hey. You up to riding double on my bike?"

Mario's eyes lit up. "You mean I can hang with you today?

Carlos nodded. "If Mama okays it. The BMX Ranch opens at eleven. Can you be ready by then?"

"Sure." Mario headed for the kitchen. "Mom!"

Carlos was reaching to turn off the television when a news alert banner popped up.

"Breaking news," said the anchor. "We've received a report of a major bee swarm attack in Douglas this morning."

Carlos's mouth went slack. He'd take a diamondback rattlesnake strike over a bee swarm sting attack. He didn't know why bees terrified him. He hated it but he couldn't help it. He was beyond afraid of bees. And everyone made fun of him for it —especially his kid brother.

"About eight this morning a man tried to remove a beehive from an old swinging bench in his backyard. The bees reacted instantaneously and chased the man onto his front porch where he collapsed. Luckily his neighbor witnessed the incident and called 911. The man was stung 100 times and has been hospitalized. Emergency crews dispatched have contained the bees. One lesson from this incident is to leave bee removal to the experts.

"Up next is John Marshall from the Arizona Department of Agriculture with tips on what to do in a bee attack."

Mario came back from the kitchen, scowling.

"What's the matter?" asked Carlos.

"Mom says I can't ride on the back of your bike. She says my leg hasn't healed."

Carlos knuckle-rubbed Mario's head. "Sorry, brother. Maybe next time."

"You still watching the stupid news?"

"Yeah. There was a bee attack In Douglas."

Mario grinned. "Buzz, buzz, buzz." He flapped his crutch-free hand in his brother's face.

"Cut it out," Carlos said, swatting his brother. "You're not funny."

"Don't think so? How about this? Roses are red, violets are blue, killer bees are coming for you." His laugh sounded like a tickled pig with hiccups. "Did you know that bears without ears are commonly referred to as B's?"

Carlos groaned.

"You smiled. I saw it."

The news was back on. "If you notice a swarm," said the Ag guy, "get inside. Close the doors and windows—"

"I have a better one," Mario said. His laugh drowned out the TV. "What do you call a bee that won't stop eating? A chub-bee."

"Buzz off. I want to hear this." Carlos turned up the volume.

"If you can't get inside," the man was saying, "pull your shirt over your head and run as fast as you can. Africanized

Honeybees can fly ten to fifteen miles per hour and will chase you the length of two football fields."

Carlos's knee started to bounce. He was a lousy runner. Maybe Mama would let him keep his bike in the house instead of the shed. On his bike, he'd have a chance to outrace them.

"What shouldn't you do if attacked?" asked the news anchor.

"Don't play dead. Don't swat at the bees."

A cramp crawled up Carlos's knee. The phone rang in the kitchen.

"Turn down the television," Mama called.

"Most important, never jump into a pool or underwater. The bees will wait until—"

Mario grabbed the remote and hit the power button.

"Hey!" Carlos said. "She said down, not off. Now I've missed it." He grabbed a couch pillow and swung it at Mario.

Mario grabbed another pillow, and the fight was on.

"mijos!" Mama stood in the doorway with her hands on her hips. "Stop this instant—before something is broken."

The boys stopped mid-swing, dropped the pillows, and did what they always did. Fake hugged. Mama fell for it every time.

"What's up?" Mario asked, grinning.

"Who called?" Carlos asked.

"Sorry. It was work. I must go in. They're short-staffed and we need the money. Carlos, you have to stay home with your brother."

"But, Mama," Carlos said, his stomach sinking. "You promised. Coach is expecting me. If you make me stay home, everyone else will get to try out the new starting ramps except me. I'll have a disadvantage on Saturday. Probably lose." He didn't add, it's not fair.

"I know," she said, "but everything costs more these days. I'm sorry, mijo. It's time for you to grow up. Paying the bills is more important than winning another bike trophy. Besides there's plenty of yard work that needs to be done."

How could she say that? Didn't she remember being thirteen? Middle school was brutal if you weren't good at something besides getting straight A's. BMX racing was the one thing he was good at. Winning made him cool. Racing trophies meant everything.

Carlos stomped outside. Why couldn't he be an only child?

He looked at their yard. Mama was right. It didn't look much better than the lot next door with its abandoned old Winnebago and condemned notice. Both yards were overgrown with scraggly weeds, had piles of uneven gravel, and looked neglected.

Even their garden shed looked junky. Summer was over but the blow-up plastic pool still rested half-in-and-half-out of the open door like someone was too lazy to take care of it properly.

He felt heat creeping up his neck.

He should help out more. His dad lived in Nogales with a new family. Carlos was the man of the family now.

Okay. He'd put things in order. It wouldn't be as nice as the Smiths'—a house with a real swimming pool across the street. Sometimes they paid him for yard work and let him swim in their pool.

He used the money to buy an old used adapted Schwinn Stingray. It wasn't even close to the top of the BMX line, but it was a start.

His friend Luis had a Haro Pro XL that Carlos would die for.

Carlos had won his trophy racing against Luis. But if Luis got to practice on the new starting ramps and Carlos didn't, Luis would be the one coming in first.

Carlos would probably end up last. He gritted his teeth. He hated being a loser. There had to be something he could do.

But what?

CHAPTER 3

Carlos looked down the dirt driveway to the street. Coyote Drive wasn't paved even though they were in a suburb of Tucson, Arizona. And that's how the locals liked it. The lots were large and covered in desert scrub. You had privacy. If you sneezed or did something else impolite, no one heard you. It felt like they lived in the country and not a city.

His gaze shifted.

Every lot had its own private desert—Palo Verde and Mesquite trees, thickets of Quail bush, Hackberry, Acacia, and bunchgrass. Plus, there were at least six different kinds of cacti to avoid bumping up against.

"Carlos!!"

His gaze swiveled to the driveway.

It was Luis. He was peddling a brand-new GT speed series black BMX bike. Back in grade school, Luis had been Carlos's best friend. Middle school changed everything. They hardly hung out at all now. BMX biking was the only time they did things together and not too often.

"Check out my new ride," Luis said, skidding to a stop. He

was dressed in the most expensive bike gear. Bike pants, a helmet, and gloves. "It's fast and light and really handles."

Carlos pretended to smile. "It's cool. But what was wrong with your Haro Pro? I thought it was your baby."

Luis shrugged. "Time for an upgrade. You should, too. Your old Schwinn has seen better days."

"It's okay. I've got it modified the way I like it."

Carlos didn't add that Luis didn't get it.

Luis's family had money. They didn't have to watch every penny spent.

Luis lived only a half-mile away from Carlos's house in a

gated subdivision across Twin Peaks Road. It was a planned neighborhood and a whole different world. The fact that Luis came from a rich family and Carlos was poor hadn't mattered until they hit Middle School.

Their friendship had changed. Carlos was a nobody. Luis had become super popular with the guys and the girls.

Stuff that hadn't mattered before now mattered big time.

Like how there was no way Carlos could afford an $800 bike. Or that Luis played first-string baseball, basketball, and soccer, ran track, and had lots of new friends. Which meant he didn't have much time for Carlos.

Mama came out dressed in her Cracker Barrel uniform. "Hi, Luis. Almost didn't recognize you. You must have grown a foot overnight. How's your mom? Haven't seen her in ages."

Luis smiled. "She's good. Dad bought her a convection oven and she's baking up a storm."

"That's nice. Well, it's off to work for me." She got into the car and rolled down the window. "Carlos, after you get the weeds cleared and the yard raked, clean out the shed." She smiled and winked. "It's nice having a man in the family. One I can rely on."

"Okay," Carlos said, wishing Mama was right. He was the man of the family. He should help out more and not complain. He'd go to the track early on Saturday and get in some practice. He couldn't win if he didn't give it his best shot.

Mario hobbled out of the house and waved his crutch at Luis. "Cool bike."

"Yeah. Can't wait for Coach to see it." Luis grinned. "Plus, Coach is bringing someone special to practice." He lowered his voice. "It's a surprise but Dad told me it's a rep from Wolf Racing. They're looking for a rider to sponsor in a new ad campaign."

Carlos's stomach dropped to his toes. Of all days, it would have to be today when he had to stay home. Life was so unfair.

"You ready to go?" Luis asked. "We'll have an hour to warm up before practice starts."

"No. I got to stay with Mario."

"Too bad. It's a one-day shot at becoming rich and famous."

Carlos shrugged and pretended he didn't care. "Mom got called into work and left me in charge."

Luis laughed. "The blind leading the blind, or as in your case —the gimp leading the gimp." He looked from one brother to the other.

Luis said it like it was a friendly joke, but Carlos knew it wasn't. It's probably what all the guys said behind his back.

Carlos pretended to laugh. "At least you have a shot at the sponsorship now."

Now it was Luis's turn to laugh awkwardly. He looked uncomfortable and stared at the open shed door with the inflated pool. "Hey, nice kiddie pool."

"Mom got it for Mario for his broken leg to do his therapy exercises." Carlos didn't add that on hot days it was great for cooling off. "Anyway, maybe I'll show up, you never know."

Luis said, "Well, don't forget Coach's rules. Text him either way or you're off the team."

Coach had put his foot down a couple of months ago when kids were showing up late or not coming to practice. He said unless his riders were serious, they were out. So now everyone had to text Coach to let him know whether they were coming or couldn't make it. And you only got one late pass. Coach had already cut two riders.

"I know," Carlos said. "I'll text him."

"Okay. See you later." Luis pushed off like he was already on the BMX Ranch track and sped down the driveway. Brutus, the neighbor's Rottweiler, appeared and raced along, barking.

Carlos grinned. For some reason, Luis was afraid of Brutus which was crazy. The old mutt just liked the attention.

"Why did you lie to Luis?" Mario asked.

"I didn't."

Mario frowned and shook his head. "Momma got the pool for us to cool off on hot days."

"Not really. She got it mainly for your physical therapy leg exercises."

"But you use it too," Mario said. Pause. "I thought you and Luis were best friends."

"We were. He has cool friends now. And I didn't lie. Just bent things a little."

Mario rolled his eyes. "Don't be mad at me. It's not my fault."

"This time it is," Carlos said bitterly.

"What did I do?"

"You were born."

Mario's face went white.

"Sorry," Carlos said. "That came out wrong."

"You hate me?" Mario's lower lip quivered.

"No, I don't. You're my brother—my best friend for life. I didn't mean it. I'm just mad. Hey! Give me five!" He held up his hand.

Mario nodded and slapped it. "I'll help with the yard. Then you can go to the practice."

Carlos shook his head. "Mama would kill me. Luis will get the sponsorship like he gets everything else. I probably didn't have a chance anyway. He's got the new bike, the looks, and a rich father."

"But you're a better rider."

Carlos grinned. "There's one thing he doesn't have. An awesome little brother like you who's really funny."

"Does that mean you want to hear another joke?"

"Sure."

"How do bees style their hair?"

"Bees don't have hair."

"With a honeycomb." Mario punched the air and gave a coyote howl.

Carlos groaned. "Hey. I need to call Coach. Can you go get my phone? It's on the couch."

"Sure." Mario headed for the house.

Carlos went to the shed where the oversized inflated pool blocked the doorway. He'd have to pull it out to get to the weed whacker. Easier said than done. By the time he'd wrestled it out the door and propped it up against the side of the shed, he was drenched in sweat. Panting, he stared into the shed and frowned.

What a mess! Cobwebs clung to the walls. Dust motes drifted aimlessly in the air. Except for his modified Schwinn bike hanging on the wall, it looked like a bomb had gone off. Carlos glanced at the broken window in the back wall. A shiver trickled down his neck as he tried to block the memory of his father smashing the glass in a fit of rage.

The shed hadn't been cleaned since. It felt like yesterday instead of two years ago.

"Shake it off," he muttered. "I am the man of this family now."

He glanced at the house. What was taking Mario so long? He must be getting a snack.

"Mario!" he shouted. "I need my phone. Stop whatever you're doing and bring it to me."

Carlos gingerly stepped into the shed and froze the instant he heard the low thrumming hum. Buzzing? Near the broken window on the back wall? Did it come from inside the shed or outside?

Holding his breath, he strained to listen but suddenly it was silent.

Had it been his imagination? The TV news story had him all freaked out.

Sweat trickled down his back and he shivered, imagining a bee crawling under his shirt.

The buzz, buzz, buzz started again, a little louder this time—a warning?

Eyes glued on the window, he stepped sideways. His foot landed on a fallen hammer and he stumbled onto the rake's tines. Its handle flew up and thwacked him in the back of the head.

"Aaaaaaagh" he yelled.

CHAPTER 4

C arlos grabbed his throbbing head and kicked the rake. "Stupid rake!"

Suddenly the shed seemed hotter and stuffier. His rake dance had stirred up the dust making his nose twitch. He sneezed—rubbed the back of his head.

"Buzz. Buzz. Buzz."

The loud buzzing morphed into hiccuped laughter.

"Mario!" Carlos spun and stumbled on the rake. Again. Arms windmilling, he fought for balance. He landed on his knees—half in and half out of the shed door. He scrambled to his feet, his heart beating like a steam pump.

"You're going to be sorry," he shouted. Race-limping, he charged around the outside of the shed.

Mario leaned against the back wall, armed with the crutch in both hands and ready for battle. He jabbed the pseudo-weapon in the air as if warding off a rabid coyote. "You can't touch me."

"Want to bet?"

"Mama will be mad if you hurt me."

Carlos grabbed the crutch, wrenched it free, and tossed it on the ground. He stepped closer. "Who said I was going to hurt you? We're going to play tickle monster."

"No!" Mario held out his hands and started to inch away.

Carlos kept a frown on his face but inside he was grinning. He might be afraid of bees, but Mario hated being tickled. "I'm the monster and you are my prey."

"Please? Don't tickle me," Mario begged. "I won't do it again. I promise."

"Never ever?"

"Never ever."

"How do I know you're just not saying that?" Carlos said.

"I won't do it again. I promise." Mario held up two fingers. "Scout's honor."

"You're not a scout."

Mario shrugged. "Please don't tickle me."

"Okay. You don't buzz and I won't tickle." Carlos grabbed Mario by the waist, lifted him, and spun in a circle. "But it's washing machine time."

At first Mario giggled and whooped. But then he cried, "Stop. I'm going to be sick."

Carlos set Mario on his feet.

"Can I ask you something? And you don't get mad?" Mario asked.

"What?"

"Why are you afraid of a tiny little bee. You could squash it in two seconds."

"And it could sting me in a nano-second. Their stingers are full of venom. People have died from bee stings."

"Have you ever been stung?" Mario said. "Mama says if you leave them alone, they'll leave you alone."

"Well I've been stung. And it hurt." Carlos held out his hand. "My phone."

Mario's smile faded. "Uh, I forgot. I'll go get it."

Carlos went back into the shed. It was still a mess. Dusty and disorganized with junk everywhere. He grabbed the weed whacker and leaned it up against the pool outside. At least the shed would look good when it was all done. He could already picture it.

He shouldn't let his little brother get to him. Mario was just a kid and as bored as Carlos was. The fact that mom had to work was neither of their faults.

If only he could get a real job and help with the bills.

He thought about the man from Wolf Racing Luis said was coming to the practice. If Carlos could get the sponsorship, not only would he have a new bike and cool new gear, but he could also help his mom with the bills. She wouldn't have to work double shifts or go in on her days off.

That left one choice: make it to practice and wow the guy. But how could he do that if he was stuck at home with Mario?

He grabbed the broom and started sweeping. By the time the floor was clean, he had the answer. He'd bribe Johnny to come over and play video games with Mario while he was at the track.

If Mama found out, she'd be mad. But she'd get over it—if they gave him the sponsorship. The commercials alone could earn him thousands of dollars. And Mama wouldn't have to work so hard.

He still had a lot to do and only one hour before he had to leave for the track.

Carlos turned into a whirling cleaning machine. He tossed screwdrivers, hammers, and wrenches into a toolbox. It went on the shelf next to some plant clippers. Then he rolled the hose in big loops and hung it on the wall.

By the time he finished, the shed looked pretty good. Not perfect but better.

The plastic inflatable pool leaned up against the outside wall. It'd be easier to store for the winter if he let the air out. For that, he'd need Mario's help.

Where was Mario?

Carlos started for the house and spotted Mario hunched in a lawn chair by the front door staring down at his lap.

"Mario! Whatever you're doing, stop. I need your help."

"In a minute." Mario waved, looking totally guilty. He slid lower in the chair like he was hiding something. "My leg hurts."

Carlos gave up on deflating the pool and went back into the shed to grab the weed whacker.

CHAPTER 5

Carlos grinned. Mama would be happy when she saw the shed.

His chores were half done. If he kept up this pace, he'd definitely make it to practice. Wait. He still hadn't texted Coach.

His grin morphed into a frown. Mario was supposed to bring him his phone. He'd better not be running down the battery playing some stupid game.

"Mario! Where's my phone?" he yelled, striding toward the house.

Halfway there, a bee dive-bombed him. A real bee, one with wings whirling—not one of his brother's pranks. Carlos's heart began to pound.

What had the news reporter said?

Cover your face and head. And run.

He yanked his T-shirt over his head and ran for the house. By the time he reached Mario, he was panting.

"Why is your shirt on your head?" Mario asked. "You look weird."

Carlos checked that the bee was gone, pulled down the shirt, and held out his hand. "My phone. Now."

"You don't have to be a jerk," Mario said. "Take it." He tossed the phone.

"Hey!" Carlos dived but his fingers grabbed air. His Samsung cell clattered on the concrete porch.

Mario's eyes went wide. "Oops. I thought you could catch."

Carlos saw red and lunged. "I asked you for my phone and you just tossed it on the cement!" He caught his brother's shirt, pulled hard. It ripped in the scuffle, but Carlos didn't let go.

"I'm sorry," Mario gasped. "I didn't mean to. I'll never touch your phone again."

"You better keep that promise." Carlos stepped back, heard an awful crunch, and felt his future disappear.

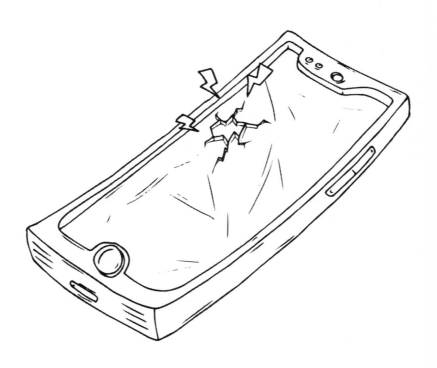

Mario's face went white. He scooted inside, shouting, "I didn't do it. It's not my fault."

With a groan, Carlos picked up his phone and heard the door slam shut. The cell's screen was black and cracked. He shook it and a piece of glass fell out.

"No. No. No. This can't be happening."

Frantically he tried to turn it on, a million thoughts racing through his head. "Please. Just work long enough for one message."

He shook the phone.

Nothing.

He collapsed into the lawn chair, defeated. This was the worst day ever. The Samsung was junk, and his life was ruined. There was no way he could text coach now. He was done—off the team for good.

Not only would he lose his spot, he'd be the only guy in middle school without a phone. Not just the kid with the limp— but a two-time loser.

His future was over. No friends. No texts. No games. No videos. And worst of all he'd miss the most important opportunity of his life if he didn't contact Coach.

On top of that, Mama would be furious. She'd spent a month's worth of tips to buy it.

"I'm done," he muttered. "Unless . . ." He breathed deep, hope lighting a tiny flame in his chest. He leaped up.

He'd use the landline to call both Coach and Johnny. He was pretty sure he had their numbers written down somewhere. Whatever it took, he was getting that sponsorship. Then he could buy the hottest cell phone. And maybe one for Mario, too.

But what if Luis won the endorsement? *Don't go there.*

At least that stupid bee was gone.

He tried the door. It was locked. Great.

"Open up," Carlos shouted, jiggling the handle. "I need to use the landline."

From inside, the television blasted cartoons.

Carlos pounded harder. "Come on. Unlock the door. I'm not mad at you. It was a stupid accident." Pause. "I'm the one who stepped on it."

Fine. If he couldn't call them, he'd modify his plan. Practice started in half an hour. He'd finish the chores, ride to Johnny's house, and convince him to come over and play video games with Mario. Then he'd book it to the track and explain everything to Coach.

Hopefully Coach would let him off the hook for not texting this one time.

He fired up the weed whacker. It was loud and vibrated his arms.

The door opened and Mario stuck his head out. "You're not going to kill me?" he shouted over the whacker's engine.

"I'm still thinking about it."

Mario started to retreat.

"Wait!" Carlos shut off the machine. "I was kidding. It was an accident."

"So you're not going to kill me?"

Carlos shook his head. "Come back out and read your comic books."

"Okay." At least Mario looked embarrassed. He held open the door. "You can use the landline."

"When I'm done here." Carlos restarted the weed whacker.

Its whirling green string tore at yellowed bunchgrass, whipping up a dirt and grass dust storm. Carlos coughed. Why hadn't he thought to grab a facemask? Sweat streamed down his cheeks leaving gritty streaks.

He made wider sweeps with the roaring whacker. Rocks flew and bounced off the side of the house while Mario sat in the yard with his boot-cast propped up on a milk crate.

Carlos worked around the side of the house until the weeds

were uprooted. Time to trade the whacker for the rake and scrape the grass into little piles.

When he'd raked the length of the house, he spotted a clump he'd missed with the weed whacker. Grabbing the clump with both hands, he pulled.

At first nothing happened.

"Stupid weed," he shouted.

He took the rake and beat at the roots like he was fighting off a rattlesnake. The ground began to crumble. That was weird. Little holes were appearing.

He squinted.

The dirt shifted. A bigger hole appeared.

And then a bee crawled out.

The striped, yellow creature looked angry. It halted near the hole's edge like a sentry and stared up at him. Two big black eyes glared, and its stinger vibrated as if ready to attack.

Carlos couldn't take his eyes off it. It was just a bee. One little bee. Standing motionless on the loose dirt.

The wings whirred. It lifted off and hovered over the open hole.

Carlos told himself not to freak out.

But then there were two. Three. Four. Shoot! He'd dug up a hive. Horror ricocheted down his spine.

Grabbing the rake, he frantically tried to cover the hole.

Panic-stricken, he stomped the ground to pack down the dirt. He had to trap the bees underground. But with each foot-fall, the ground crumbled a little more. Another bee pushed through the loose dirt.

"Shoot!" He was making things worse.

Carlos threw the rake down and ran for the front door. They had to get inside before the bees could swarm and attack.

"Into the house," Carlos shouted to Mario. "Move."

"Quit bossing me around." Mario turned the page of his comic. "I'm reading." He looked up and smiled. "I got you a glass of water."

Carlos looked back over his shoulder. More bees had emerged. They were forming a low, black buzzing cloud just inches off the ground. Soon they would be airborne. There wasn't time to argue. Carlos pulled but Mario didn't budge. His boot cast was snagged on the chair.

"Hey." Mario tried to jerk free. "That hurts. Are you trying to break my leg again?"

"No. I'm trying to save your life," Carlos said, panting out each word. "There's a swarm of bees. They're coming."

"A swarm of bees?" Mario laughed but when he turned his eyes widened. "BEES!" For the first time he looked scared.

Carlos grasped the doorknob, turned it, and yanked. And yanked it again. It was locked. He started to hyperventilate.

"Tell me you have the house keys in your pocket."

CHAPTER 6

Carlos stared through the window. The house keys hung on their usual hook under the wall phone.

He whipped his head back to the bee cloud. It wasn't moving. Yet. But it was twice the size, hovering just over the rake he'd left in the dirt. There had to be hundreds of bees. Maybe a thousand. Or more.

For some reason, they hadn't followed him to the house. Didn't they see him run? Or had they identified the rake as the enemy?

"What are we going to do?" Mario squeaked.

"We have to find another way in," Carlos whispered. "Get low and cover your head. Be ready to run."

As Mario scrunched down and pulled his shirt over his face, Carlos threw his shoulder against the door to pop the lock.

The door didn't budge. He slammed it again. And again. After two more tries, his shoulder hurt and they were still outside with the bees.

Even worse, hitting the door had got the bees' attention. The dark bee cloud distorted into a noise-seeking missile. It swarmed toward where the boys huddled.

They had to get inside.

Carlos's mind raced. The windows. Maybe one of them was unlocked.

The swarm shot over the covered porch, scouring the air and searching for the enemy.

Carlos put a finger to his lips. Maybe if he and Mario moved super slow, they could get away.

The neighbor's Rottweiler started to bark. The swarm swooped toward the dog's howls.

Thank you, Brutus.

"Mario!" Carlos whispered. "I'll try the living room window. Keep low and don't move. I don't think they've figured out we're here."

Carlos crept along the side of the house and heaved up on the nearest window. It didn't budge.

What now? Should they run?

"The bees are coming back," Mario whispered. "Break the window so we can get inside."

"No, then they'll be able to get in, too. I'll try the kitchen window. Follow me and stay close."

He tiptoed to it with Mario hobbling behind. It was locked too.

Shoot.

The bee cloud had reached the giant saguaro cactus by the drive.

Think!

The house was out. That left one option. Not a great one but what other choice did they have?

"Run for it. That way. Go."

"I can't run," Mario whimpered. "My leg." He turned to face the swarm, raising his crutch like a baseball bat. "I'll swat 'em all."

"Forget that." Carlos threw the crutch down, slung Mario over his shoulder, and ran for the shed.

Mario's started screeching. "The swarm looks like a giant fastball. It's coming straight at us."

"Shut up," Carlos panted. Mario was heavier than he looked. "You're making things worse."

Mario's grasp tightened and Carlos's foot twisted. Pain raced up his shorter leg but he kept going. He had to get Mario to safety. They were almost there. Just another six feet to go. Five. Four. Three. Two.

They'd reached the shed.

He dropped Mario onto his feet and yanked open the door. The blood pumping through his heart had given him super strength—too much. He ripped the door open. Now the shed door dangled on one hinge. So much for his escape plan.

A sharp stabbing sensation pierced his neck. Uh oh. The first bee had located them. Without looking, he knew the swarm was close behind.

Time was running out.

The sting throbbed a million times worse than any sting he'd ever had. And it wasn't his imagination. These weren't regular bees. These were killer bees!

"Quick. Drop flat on the ground. And keep your face covered."

"No. We have to run," Mario argued.

"You're too slow and you're too heavy for me to carry." Carlos shoved Mario down. "Just do what I tell you."

"We're going to die," Mario cried. "They'll swarm us and sting us all over. And we'll die."

"Lay flat. Don't move. I have another idea."

Carlos scrambled to the side of the shed where he'd propped the big, rectangular, inflatable swimming pool earlier. It was semi-clear, and the sun shone through the red, white, and blue colors. The plastic pool might only be three feet deep, but it was wide enough to hold six.

"What are you doing?"

"Head down," Carlos ordered, grabbing the pool and flipping it topside over his brother like a giant shield.

The swarm buzzed like an air brigade, setting his heart racing. He took one last look and dove under the pool.

They were safe—for the moment.

"Carlos? Will the pool keep the bees out?"

"Yeah," Carlos said, hoping it was true. "I don't think they can chew through plastic." His skin prickled. Not plastic, but what about dirt?

"You better be right." Mario sucked in a big breath. "How long until they leave us alone?"

Carlos's stomach began to twist into knots.

The bees had built their hive in the ground. They knew how to dig and burrow. How far did their tunnels go? Were they safe hiding under this cheap swimming pool on the ground?

CHAPTER 7

Carlos and Mario lay on their sides, sweat soaking their skin. They faced each other under the red, white, and blue plastic pool. It was like a sauna—hot and the air thick. Mario was still panting through his open mouth.

"Chill and breathe through your nose," Carlos said, wiping sweat from his face. "Or you're going to use up all our oxygen."

"When are they going to leave?"

Waiting for the bees to get tired and leave didn't seem to be working. Instead of going away, more had arrived. The bee-cloud looked larger and darker, and now he could clearly hear a buzzing hum. Several had settled on the pool and had become dark spots crawling across the plastic pool overhead.

"Are those bees?" Mario asked.

Carlos nodded.

Mario slapped the pool. The bees took flight.

"Don't," Carlos said. "You're only making them angry."

"I thought you said we're safe under here."

"We are." At least I hope we are, he added to himself. "And now they know we're still here."

"Oh." Mario fell silent.

The bees returned and resumed their search for the pool's weakness. More winged avengers joined them. The buzzing multiplied. Shifting shadows intent on revenge. They were like storm clouds morphing from one ominous image to another.

Carlos squeezed his eyes shut. Five minutes passed.

"I'm tired of being stuck under here," Mario complained. "The ground's hard. My leg hurts. This was a stupid plan."

"Maybe. But we're still alive."

"Why don't they go away?" Mario complained. "We've been under here forever. Maybe longer and I'm thirsty."

"It's probably only been ten minutes," Carlos said. "Waiting a little longer won't kill you." He didn't add, but the bees will. There was no point in getting Mario riled up again. Complaining Mario was easier to deal with than panicked Mario.

"How many stings do you have?" Mario said. "I have six."

"Ten. I think," Carlos said. "Not enough to be dangerous." He didn't add, and they're still throbbing.

A vehicle blasting with country and western music stopped at the end of their drive—engine idling.

"Wahoo," he shouted, hope bursting like fireworks in a Fourth of July night sky.

It had to be the mail carrier. He always listened to that kind of cheating-heart music.

Grinning, Carlos pushed Mario's shoulder.

They were going to make it.

"Yell. Get his attention." Carlos rose onto his elbows. "HELP! Bee attack! We're under the pool."

Mario joined in. "Call 9-1-1."

The mail truck's engine shifted into gear.

"Noooooooooo," shouted Carlos. His grin slipped.

"Don't go," Mario whispered. "We need help."

Carlos kept yelling. Louder. "Come back." He kept at it until his throat was sore and his voice croaked.

No one was coming.

He was mad at himself. Why hadn't he thought of the mail carrier earlier? He and Mario could have crawled out to the road. Waited. Been rescued. But it was too late now.

Carlos realized Mario must be totally frightened because his little brother had rolled onto his side. He was chewing his lip and silent tears mingled with the sweat on his cheeks.

Above the pool, the bees were going crazy, stirred up by all the shouting. They seethed in a death dance atop the plastic. The swarm had grown into a blanket so thick that they blotted out the sun.

Lying in their shadow, Carlos felt ill. No one was coming to help. It would be hours before Mama got home. His next thought sent a chill into his heart. By then, the bees would have burrowed under the pool's edge and stung them a thousand times.

His hand slid over the swollen welts on his arms and face. He squinted through the plastic at the dark, ever-changing swarm. If there had been a thousand bees before, there must be ten thousand now. Their weight pressed down on the plastic, making it sag.

Carlos looked at Mario and dry swallowed, wishing he had a big brother to protect him. But that was his job. Mama expected him to take care of Mario and keep him safe.

Okay. Time to think. What did he know about bee attacks?

Bees can fly ten to fifteen miles per hour.

If you see a bee swarm, protect your face.

Run away as fast as you can.

Don't swat at the bees.

Don't play dead.

Never jump into a pool to hide underwater.

It all sounded easy unless you were a bee hostage.

All the advice in the world was no good if it didn't help. He and Mario were stuck under a plastic blow-up swimming pool, hot, thirsty, and with no help on the way.

It was time to man up. If they were going to survive, it was up to Carlos to come up with a real plan.

CHAPTER 8

The hovering swarm cast an even larger and darker shadow over the pool. Carlos imagined there must be thousands of bees in the pulsating blob. He was confident the bees couldn't chew through the plastic shield, but now they seemed to search every inch of it, looking for a way in.

His gaze shifted.

Some bees had started crawling down the pool's outer wall, just inches from his face. How long would it take for them to discover a bee-sized crack between the plastic and the ground?

He shivered, his sweat burning like acid, and glanced at Mario.

Mario was on his stomach and focused on drawing a giant wasp in the dirt with his finger. Obviously, his little brother hadn't noticed the bees searching for an entrance along the ground or he'd be chewing his lip again.

That was good. At least drawing kept him busy, giving Carlos time to think. He started running through options, trying to devise a workable plan.

Escape idea one: wait for the bees to get tired and fly away.

His jaw clenched. The swarm wasn't leaving. Some bees covered the pool's surface while others flew in frantic circles. It was only a matter of time before they wriggled under the pool's flimsy plastic edge.

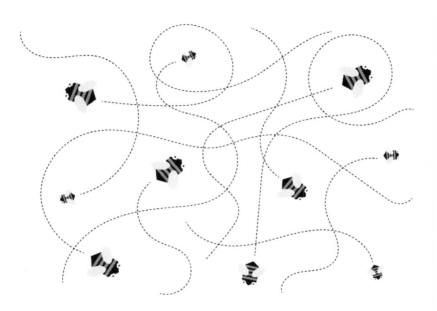

Carlos and Mario would be trapped in a stinging nightmare.

His teeth clamped together so tight it hurt. He forced himself to relax his jaw muscles and breathe deep. Focus on surviving not. . . the other.

Escape idea two: run like the news reporter suggested. Carlos shook his head. The instant they tossed the pool covering aside, the bees would be all over them like two massive blankets. Plus, Mario had a broken leg and Carlos was too slow with his shorter leg. He'd be even slower if he had to carry Mario. Running wouldn't work.

Escape idea three . . .

Nothing came.

Frantic, Carlos squinted at the droning enemy. The noise was unbelievable. How could the swarm be growing bigger? He dry-swallowed.

Think.

Think.

Think.

A memory popped into his head.

They were in front of their house. Mario was pitching and Carlos was swinging an aluminum bat. After twenty strikes, Carlos grand-slammed the baseball into the neighbor's lot. Cacti, brush, and Palo Verdi trees studded the ramshackle yard. The owners had abandoned it ages ago. The only sign they'd once lived there was an old RV camper.

The brothers hadn't found the ball, but the RV had been unlocked and they'd peeked inside.

Now, Carlos shook his fist at the bees. He had a plan.

They'd use the pool as a shell, play snail, and crawl to the rusty RV. Then they'd get inside and wait out the bees until Mama came home.

"Why are you grinning?' Mario asked.

"I have an idea. But it will only work if you do exactly what I say this time. Can I count on you?"

Mario stared at the dirt and nodded. "I wish everything wasn't my fault."

"It's not," Carlos said, even though most of it was Mario's fault, but that didn't matter now. "I stepped on my phone. You didn't."

"Yeah, but I threw it."

"And I stepped on it." Pause. "And worse, I weed-whacked the beehive."

"I locked the keys in the house," Mario sniffled.

"Forget it. We both messed up. Now it's time to be a lean, mean, bee-fighting team." He raised his fist for a knuckle bump.

Mario returned a half-hearted knuckle slap.

"We have amigo power. We're smarter than a bunch of bees," Carlos said. "I know exactly what we have to do."

"What?" Mario sounded a little less scared.

"Escape idea numeral tres." Carlos took a deep breath and hoped Mario wouldn't be freaked out when he heard the plan. It was crazy but it might just work. "Do you think you can crawl?"

CHAPTER 9

"Are you sure this is a good idea?" Mario said, eyeing the heavy, menacing swarm. "Why don't they leave?"

Carlos wiped his forehead. "The news guy said killer bees stay in attack mode for a long time. Sometimes hours. This pool won't protect us forever."

"I don't want to go." Mario pinched his lips and hummed a long, single note in unison with the bees. *"Hmmmmmm."*

"Come on, buddy, we can do this." He tried not to look at the growing layer along the ground.

"It stinks being stuck under here." Mario's face was drenched with sweat and his hair was plastered to his head.

"That's why we need to get moving. I don't want to wait five hours until Mama gets home. Besides, the only thing that stinks is your armpits."

"Not funny." Mario bared his teeth like a pit bull. "Your idea is stupid. I'm hot. And I want Mama. And I'm dying of thirst."

"Think of something else. If you're thirsty we need to get moving."

Mario ignored him.

"I mean it. We need to go."

Mario pinched his lips and started to hum. "Hmmmmmm." At first, he was in unison with the bee chorus, holding onto a long, single note. It sounded eerie. The bees didn't seem to notice. Then Mario's head began to bob, and he hummed a loud bouncy rhythm. His shoulders rocked and his fingers tapped along.

The bees went crazy. The swarm split into chaos and then reformed to dive-bomb the pool. The impact vibrated the plastic.

Mario's mouth and eyes popped open in terror.

Carlos's pulse pounded in his ears. "Let's go. Grab your side. Keep it down. We need to get to the abandoned RV."

Carlos belly-crawled to the front of the pool. He glanced at his brother. Mario hadn't moved. He seemed petrified—his eyes were locked on the teeming mass of winged avengers.

"Mario! Snap out of it. We've got to move. Get on your stomach."

"The bees are everywhere," Mario whispered but did as he was told.

"We'll go slow. Make sure your side stays on the ground. I'll do the same."

Carlos kept his elbows on the hard dirt and held down the pool's front edge. "Ready?"

"Ready."

"Okay. Tell me if you need to stop. Uno. Dos. Tres. Now."

Crawling on his elbows, Carlos used his hands to inch the pool forward.

The swarm seemed confused. It soared upward in a massive black cloud. Then it resumed its deadly vigil, landing and busily searching the pool's surface.

The brothers kept moving.

They'd only traveled for about three minutes when Mario said, "How long will this take? We're moving like snails. And the bees are having no problem keeping up."

Carlos didn't bother answering. His brother's complaining was a good sign. It meant he wasn't as scared as before.

"Mama's not going to like this. My cast is filling with dirt."

"You can take it off and dump it when we get inside the RV. Just keep moving. Make sure no bees get in. If you see one, squash it."

"With what?"

"Your fist."

"Eew!" Mario said. "Are we there yet?"

"Almost."

Stones scattered under their hands and knees. They reached

the property line. Carlos halted. Only twenty feet lay between them and the rusted Winnebago Minnie Winnie.

Unfortunately, those twenty feet contained screwbean mesquite, hackberry brush, and thorny cacti. There was no straight path. They were growing so close together, he felt sick.

How would they get through?

Everything looked distorted through the double layers of plastic. He knew well-worn animal trails looped right and left. Were they wide enough for the pool? He wasn't sure. Which was crazy. He'd lived his whole life next door to the lot but hadn't paid attention.

"Why'd you stop?" Mario asked.

"I'm deciding which way to go."

"And?"

"We'll turn right first and then double back. There's a wider path for the pool that way." He crossed his fingers and prayed he'd made the best choice. "It won't take more than an extra few minutes."

The killer bee cloud churned with their ominous, never-ending hum. They seemed to be waiting for him to make a mistake. They must smell them under the pool. He wished he'd never used the weed whacker and had woken them up. Why couldn't they just leave?

He spotted a wide gap in the desert scrub. What a relief. It was an old, rutted road, leading into the property. They eased onto it and scooted faster now that they had a clear path.

"Won't be long now," Carlos gasped and pushed forward, ignoring his scraped hands and knees.

The pool bumped into something.

"No!" The word escaped before Carlos could stop it. Not now. They were almost to the RV.

"What's that hissing noise?" Mario cocked his head to the side. A bee's shadow crawled over his face. "It sounds like a rattlesnake."

"No snake," Carlos assured his brother. "We got too close to a jumping Cholla cactus."

"What now?" Mario cried. The pool was deflating by the second.

"Keep going. Crawl a little faster."

"I am," Mario sobbed.

Carlos knew his kid brother's leg had to be hurting and that his palms and knees had to be shredded. "Almost there, you've got this."

Soon they were draped in a semi-clear red, white, and blue plastic shroud, which was blanketed with killer bees. The whole mass hung heavily on their backs.

They squirmed onward.

It was hard to see through the plastic, but Carlos spotted the RV just ahead—only five feet left to go.

Then, like some miracle, they were there.

The Winnebago might be an old, abandoned RV camper but it looked like a palace.

"I told you we'd make it," Carlos said.

"So did the bees," Mario squeaked. "I just thought of something. What if it's locked like the house?"

"It's not."

"How do you know?" Mario demanded suspiciously.

"We looked inside, remember?"

"But that was a long time ago, and—"

"Listen to me. We'll jump up as fast as we can. We'll keep the pool on us until I get the door open. Then we'll dive inside and slam the door. Got it?"

Mario bit his lip and nodded.

"Okay. Ready?" Carlos paused, praying they weren't stung too many times before they got into the RV. "Now!"

CHAPTER 10

Together, the brothers threw the pool with its mass of bees backward and dove inside.

Chest heaving, Carlos slammed the RV door shut. He leaned up against the wall to catch his breath, gulping in the stale, musty air.

"We did it. That was close," Carlos gasped.

The brothers grinned at each other.

Mario limped a few feet, wincing, and plopped down on a paint can. Carlos pressed his raw palms against his legs to stop their burning.

They were in the kitchen. Everything looked half-sized, like it was built for a hobbit—a two-burner stove, a tiny sink, and a refrigerator barely large enough to hold a grocery sack.

Once, it must have been nice with its wood-paneled walls and built-in cabinets. Now it was a dump, littered with old stuff. Carlos counted eight bulging black plastic bags. He peeked in one. At least it wasn't rotting garbage. Just junk. Old tape. Papers. Broken odds and ends. And who knew what else.

"This place is a pit," Mario said. "Do you think the old guy was a hoarder?"

Carlos shrugged. "Don't know. Don't care. We're safe." He pulled open the kitchen drawer and slammed it shut. It looked like mice had used it for a toilet. The cabinets weren't much better.

Mario stared at one of the windows. "You sure we're safe?"

Carlos nodded and hoped it was the truth.

Outside, the muted buzzing was a throbbing reminder that the bees were in attack mode. Did they ever give up? He knew the answer was no—at least not for a good while. That's what made killer bees so famous. And deadly. They darkened the windows, crawling and searching for cracks or gaps.

Carlos scanned the room to make sure none had gotten in.

The coast was clear.

Anyway, he'd know by now if they'd found a crack—they would have already attacked.

All they had to do was sit there until Mama got home.

"I thought your plan was stupid," Mario said. "But you know what? That was awesome."

"Stick with me and we'll be good."

Mario rolled his eyes, grinning. Then his grin morphed into a frown. "Wait, what if the bees are still here when Mama comes looking for us? They'll attack her."

Carlos shook his head. "She won't be home for at least five hours. The bees will be long gone before then."

Carlos hoped his words were true.

"What if Mama phones on her break to check on us?" Mario asked.

That would be a disaster. They couldn't answer and she'd think something was wrong.

"Don't worry," Carlos said, hoping he spoke the truth. "We'll be out of here by the time Spiderman comes on at three. I'll even watch it with you."

Of all days to break his phone? The one time there was an emergency, he didn't have it. They could have called for help. He could have texted Coach. Now Coach had to think he was a flake. He'd be off the team. And so much for impressing the Wolf Racing sponsor. He pushed the thoughts from his mind. The only thing to worry about now was surviving.

"I'm bored," Mario said.

"Already?"

"This place is small. I wouldn't want to live here. There's no bed."

"That's because the bedroom door is shut."

Mario's head swiveled. "Door? Where?"

Carlos pointed. "Right behind you. It's a pocket door. It slides into the wall."

Mario stood awkwardly on his cast and hopped toward the sliding partition. "Wow. It looks just like the wall. Sort of."

Carlos grinned. Mario was a mess—sweat-streaked, dirty, and scratched. A red welt had sprouted on Mario's cheek and another on his neck.

"What's so funny?" Mario said, plopping down on his paint can.

"I wonder if I look as bad as you do?"

"Worse."

They both laughed.

Now that the danger was over, his adrenaline rush faded. He winced. Throbbing pain sprouted on his forehead, arms, belly, and legs.

"How many?" Carlos rubbed his arm and flinched.

"How many what?" Mario said, suddenly looking like he was going to barf.

"How many stings do you have?"

Mario grew pale and peeled up his shirt. "Oh no. One, two, three, four, five, six. Am I going to die?"

"No. But you didn't count the one on your face and neck.

Seven." Carlos tried to put on a brave face and examined himself. "Beat you. I have ten and I'm not dead."

The welts hurt but not as bad as when Carlos had wrecked his bike and road-rashed his whole leg. "Don't worry. We'll be fine if we don't get stung again. They aren't swelling, are they?"

"No, but they hurt," Mario said.

"They'll stop hurting soon. Promise."

"Do you know the worst part about getting stung by bees?" Mario said, looking serious.

"The itchy pain?"

"No," Mario giggled. "Now we have to take care of their hives."

Carlos stifled a snort and wondered if bee venom had messed up his little brother's mind. "What are you talking about?"

"It's a joke. Don't you get it? The little red bumps that look like zits where the bees stung you. They're hives. We've got them. And we have to deal with them."

Carlos groaned and rolled his eyes. At least Mario was back to himself, corny jokes and all. "How's your leg?"

Mario shrugged. "It's okay." He held up one arm. "But my arm is covered in dried blood and dirt."

"Maybe I should take the first shower tonight because all your dirt will clog the pipes," Carlos said. "And Mama will have to call a plumber. And I'll have to wait for morning to get cleaned up."

"At least my jokes are funny," Mario said, smiling. He rooted through a pile and held up a huge, twisted ball of wire and a Marie Callender pie tin. "Why did they leave all this junk? It's just garbage."

"That's why. They didn't want to take it," Carlos said. "But hey, there is some good stuff. Duct tape. Lots of old newspapers to read."

Mario made a face.

"With comic strips."

"Hand 'em over," Mario said.

Carlos grabbed an armful, dropped them next to Mario, and went back to rummaging.

"Cool. This is something we really need." Carlos held up a deflated soccer ball. It was flat as a pancake and just as floppy. "Want to play soccer?"

"I don't know," Mario said with mock seriousness. "We're not supposed to horse around inside 'cause something might get broken." He grinned. "Plus, I can't kick the ball with a broken foot."

"Yeah, but you can bounce it off your head." Carlos flung it like a Frisbee. It sailed past Mario and hit the pocket door.

Thwack. The door shifted. A tiny crack appeared.

The bees outside went wild. The window crawlers took flight.

The buzzing grew louder. Closer. Like the bees were in the Winnebago with them.

Weird.

"Carlos?" Mario's voice sounded strained. "Look."

On the floor, a single bee was crawling through the tiny crack in the pocket door.

CHAPTER 11

The bee didn't hesitate. Before Carlos could react, it shot straight at him. Adrenaline kicked in and Carlos grabbed a filthy red handkerchief and shoved it into the crack. Ignoring the sharp sting on his neck, he kept working until the crack was filled.

"Ouch!" Another sting. Carlos slapped his cheek fast and hard. In his palm, the bee was smashed. He shook it off and stepped on it. He knew that crushed bees gave off an alarm scent that sent other bees into a frenzy, but he'd had no choice.

"Carlos," Mario cried. "Something's in my cast. Ow. Ow! It stung me."

"Should I take off your cast?" Carlos said. The temporary boot cast was supposed to be on for one more week.

"Get it off. Get it off." Mario was freaking out big time. His eyes were wide with terror, and he kept slapping at his leg.

"Okay. Give me a second." Carlos dropped to his knees and pulled on the Velcro straps holding the boot cast in place.

"Hurry," Mario said, wincing at the ripping sound. "Before it stings me again."

Carlos peeled the temporary boot cast open. Mario's leg looked awful pale and skinny. Getting the bee without re-injuring his brother would be tricky.

Mario started hyperventilating.

"Where is it?" Carlos asked.

"Under my knee." Mario's leg jerked. "Ow. It stung me again." He swatted his leg with both hands.

Carlos grabbed Mario's arms. "Stop. I'll lift your leg and see if I can knock it off."

Tears flooded Mario's face.

The bee crawled onto Mario's kneecap.

"Don't move," Carlos said. "I'll get it."

Cupping his hand over the vibrating bee, he swiped it to the floor. Then grabbed an old tennis shoe and hammered the bee like he was driving a nail. The bee was history.

"You okay?" Carlos said.

Mario nodded. "But my leg hurts."

"Sorry, I didn't mean to hurt you."

"You didn't. The bee did." He rubbed his hand over his knee. "I think it got me three times before you knocked it off."

"Well, it won't ever sting you again."

Mario half grinned through his tears. "Hey. Look at the windows. The bees are gone. They gave up!"

"Maybe," Carlos said, breathing deep and letting it out slow. "Or they got tired after we outsmarted them and buzzed off. Either way, we're safe. No more running. No more crawling. Best of all, no more stings."

"So, we can get out of this dump, pronto," Mario said, struggling to stand.

"Not yet," Carlos said. "Sit down."

"What do you mean? Not yet?" Mario's lips pinched into a line.

"Let's give the bees plenty of time to retreat to their hive."

"You said they can fly ten miles an hour. If that's true, they should already be there."

"Yeah, but what if there's a straggler? It would only take one bee to raise the alarm and bring back the whole swarm. We need to wait at least fifteen minutes. Maybe more. You don't want to be stung again. Do you?"

Mario plopped down on his paint can, rubbing his sore leg. "What are we going to do for fifteen minutes?"

"I don't know," Carlos said. "How about you tell me a joke." Telling jokes were guaranteed to keep his kid brother distracted.

Mario's eyes sparkled. "Got one and I bet you can't guess it. Why did the bee lose his job at the barber shop?"

Carlos forced his eyes not to roll. "Don't you know any jokes that aren't about bees?"

"Because the bee only gave buzz-cuts." Mario giggled. "Even to the girls. Can you imagine Maggie Titus with a bald head?"

The joke was bad. Corny. Juvenile. Maybe it was the adrenaline. Laughter burst from Carlos's lungs, loud and raucous. He couldn't stop. Mario joined and the two of them howled like a pair of coyotes celebrating a full moon.

As quickly as it had started, it stopped.

Mario spoke first. "I told you it was funny. Can we go now?"

"Wait a second," Carlos said. "Shh, I think I hear something."

A sickly sensation of bees crawling in his hair sent prickles of fear racing to his toes. He could hear them. Maybe he was paranoid.

"What is it?" Mario demanded.

Carlos held up his hand.

The old red handkerchief stuffed in the crack seemed to quiver. Was it his imagination or was the rag alive? Then it stopped. Breathing in and out. But that was impossible.

"Did you see that?" Carlos said.

"I didn't see anything."

"I don't think they left. I think they're all in the front room of the RV—on the other side of the pocket door."

Like something out of a horror movie, the handkerchief popped into the room. Two winged intruders slipped through. Carlos leaped to his feet and plugged the hole.

"Toss me that duct tape," Carlos said. "Hurry."

"Where is it?" Mario said. "I don't see it."

Carlos frantically pressed the handkerchief over the hole, ignoring two sharp stings to his neck.

"Behind you. On the floor."

"I found something better. Hey, mean old bees," Mario taunted. "Come this way. Over here."

"Just give me the tape," Carlos shouted.

Mario tossed it and Carlos snagged it mid-air, ripped off a length and spun back to the door. "Cover your face, Mario. Quit messing around."

The tape was old and a little gooey sticky, but it would work. Carlos slapped the tape strip over the rag and tore off another piece. Another strip and another until silver tape completely covered the red handkerchief. Almost done.

A *psssssst* sound came from behind his back, accompanied by the scent of oil. He ignored it and focused on pressing the tape's edges to the door. Finally, the dangerous gap was sealed off.

That should hold them for a while.

Dreading what Mario had been up to, Carlos turned to look at his little brother.

CHAPTER 12

Expecting the worst, Carlos stared, his worry morphing into a grin.

Mario held a blue and yellow can of WD40.

"That's what I smelled. What were you doing with it?"

"I sprayed the bees," Mario said, "and they just dropped. See?" He poked at two oil-drenched bees on the floor with a broken pencil. They weren't moving. Mario slammed the can down on them for good measure. "Take that. Your stinging days are over."

"Good job," Carlos said. "We're safe for now. Let's put your walking cast back on. Might as well be ready if we have to run."

"Run? Why? You just said we were safe."

"We are if the bees stay on their side of the door."

Mario scowled. "Stupid bees. How did they even get inside?"

"I think I know. Remember when I hit a grand slam off your pitch?"

"When you lost my best baseball with a lucky hit? Yeah."

"I searched all over," Carlos said. "Except for in this RV's front room. I bet you twenty pancakes it's in there."

Mario groaned. "Can't you close the pocket door tighter?"

Carlos shook his head. "Something's wrong with it. And if I try to fix it, I'll probably make things worse. I'll help you put the cast back on."

"Do I have to?" Mario said. "We're just sitting here and it kind of feels good to have it off."

Carlos nodded. "Mama would want you to."

Mario made a face but grabbed the cast and put it on.

"Happy now?" Mario said.

"Think you can stand on it?" Carlos said.

"I think so."

"I'll help and you can see if it feels right. Okay?"

Carlos helped his brother up.

Mario put his weight on the walking cast and winced.

"Too loose?" Carlos said.

"No. The cast is rubbing my bee stings. Now they itch and hurt at the same time."

"Think of something else."

"Like what? The bees buzzing in the walls and up there?" Mario pointed at the ceiling.

The low hum coming from the walls and overhead seemed louder.

Carlos noticed a metal air vent set into the ceiling and gulped. Its little slats were the perfect size for killer bees to crawl through. The vent looked closed but everything else in this RV was broken. What if it was busted, too? What if the bees discovered it?

Scrambling, he piled a rusted metal crate on top of another one and climbed up. "Toss me the Tape. I need to get this sealed."

In a few minutes, the vent matched the door. Duct-tape Décor by Carlos!

He hopped down and put his ear to the wall. The buzzing vibrated and sounded even more ominous. Was it his imagination, or were they gnawing the wood paneling?

They couldn't stay there. Eventually, the bees would get in.

Carlos grabbed one of the full garbage bags and dumped it on the floor.

"What are you doing now?" Mario asked.

"I'm forming a new plan. A better one." Carlos crossed his fingers and prayed it would work. It was a long shot.

"Another plan?" Mario whined. "Let's just wait here. I'm tired of new plans."

Carlos stirred one foot through the garbage. It was a real pile of junk, like you'd find at a dump. Empty oil cans, squashed boxes, discarded brushes, old clothes, shoes, and hats. Broken pencils and pens, yellowed newspapers and magazines, squashed soda bottles, stuffed toys, tools, batteries, balls of wadded tin foil, and who knew what else.

Mario said, "Your plan better not be running. My crutches are back at the house."

Carlos looked at his little brother.

Mario wore his stubborn frown. "The bees can fly ten miles an hour. I can't run that fast even if I had crutches. And neither can you."

Carlos stopped rummaging. "You won't have to run."

"Well, I vote to stay here." Mario crossed his arms. "Humph."

"We can't fight off the bees if they get in." Carlos tried to sound patient. "I think they crawled into the ceiling. If they can chew dirt, they can chew wood paneling."

Mario's eyes darted upward and he paled.

"We're getting out of here." Carlos returned his attention to the garbage. "But we've got to be smart about it."

"By going through garbage?"

"We need supplies. Stuff we can use to escape."

"Like what?"

Carlos grabbed a full bag, untied its top, and dumped it in front of Mario. "Look for something we can use for a knife."

Mario used a white-stained paint stick to stir through the pile. "How about this?" He handed Carlos a broken scissor.

"Perfect." Carlos sliced the garbage bags into four large sheets and set them aside.

"What are they for?"

"Bee armor. Look for anything that might prevent bee stings." Carlos held up three Chobani yogurt cups. "These can keep bees out of your ears."

"Gross!" Mario held up a large, faded-pink-camo baseball cap. "I'll use this."

"Okay. Keep looking for more stuff."

His plan was coming together. It was risky but could work if Mario didn't freak out. And if he could trick the bees into thinking they were still inside after they slipped away.

At least long enough to make their escape.

Under the next bulging bag, Carlos found a big box coated in grime. Sitting it on the sink, he opened it and smiled. With a little luck and perhaps a prayer, this could be the plan's missing link.

CHAPTER 13

"So what's this big plan?" Mario asked.

"I'll tell you the details when you need, to know," Carlos said. It was risky and there was no point telling his brother too soon. He'd be freaked.

"That's what I thought. You don't really have one."

"Just keep looking."

Carlos pulled the ancient radio from the dusty box. It was ancient—like from the 90s with round knobs. Turning one produced a click. But no sound. He tried again. Shook it. Still nothing. Flipping it over, he found the empty slot for AAA batteries.

"Mario. Did you see any batteries?"

Mario shrugged. "I don't know. Maybe. I wasn't looking for batteries. You said to find something useful like more tape or another hat. You didn't say anything about batteries."

"Look for some," Carlos said, trying not to sound desperate. "I'll check the cupboards and drawers. Again." This time his search had a purpose. Earlier when he'd looked it had been curiosity.

The kitchen drawers were empty, except for mouse poop. Good thing he didn't have to stick his hand in there.

The cupboards were next. He put his ear to one little door and listened for buzzing.

"What are you doing? Mario asked.

"Listening for bees."

"And?" Mario bit his lip.

"Don't hear any." Carlos opened the first cupboard door. "Keep looking for batteries."

While they searched, Carlos kept an eye on the duct-taped door and vent.

"I found one," Mario shouted, holding up a D battery. "It looks too big for the radio."

"It's a start. Keep looking."

Carlos opened the last cupboard. Inside was a stuffed bear clutching little brass cymbals. This toy was going to be worth its weight in gold. Luis had one in kindergarten. Carlos had been jealous. It wobbled and banged the cymbals to kiddy music when you turned it on.

"Wahoo," Mario said. "Check it out. JACKPOT." He dumped a pile of batteries onto the floor. Big ones and little ones.

Carlos set the bear in the sink and studied the batteries. Some had gray dust and had started to corrode. Hopefully, they weren't all dead. He sorted out the AAA's and came up with eight.

"All we need are two good ones," Carlos said, trying to sound upbeat. The first four were useless. "Four down and four to go. Cross your fingers, Mario."

Carlos slid the next two into the slot. Magically the radio blared Mariachi music.

Mario started shoulder-dancing and humming to the music.

Carlos shut off the radio.

"Why did you turn it off?"

"We don't know how long the batteries will last. Plus, the noise attracts the bees." Carlos opened the back of the toy bear. "This guy takes C batteries."

Mario handed him six.

Carlos went through the same trial-and-error process. He was down to the last two batteries when the bear came to life. It banged the cymbals in time to the song, Who let the dogs out? Woof. Woof, woof.

"Cool." Mario continued to sing after the bear stopped.

Carlos did a quick inventory. Six black plastic sheets, two-and-a-half rolls of silver duct tape, three pie tins, plastic cups, the gross Chobani yogurt cups, one baseball cap, a squashed cowboy hat, and gloves.

"We're ready for phase two," Carlos said.

"What's phase two?" Mario said.

"That's when we armor up."

CHAPTER 14

Carlos grabbed two black plastic sheets and pointed to the rusty crate. "Sit on that and stretch out your legs."

"Why?" Mario asked.

"Just do it." Carlos knelt and wrapped one plastic sheet around Mario's good leg. "Hold this until I get it taped."

He wound silver tape around the leg, sealing the edges.

"Hey, you're turning me into a garbage bag mummy and it's not even Hallowe'en," Mario joked.

Carlos rolled his eyes and sealed off any holes with more tape. He took extra care with Mario's injured leg. "Legs done. Hold out your arms."

"I hope nobody sees me," Mario said, laughing. "I look stupid."

"This is the perfect armor to ward off a bee's stingers. If it makes you feel any better, I'll look just as stupid."

"I'm already sweating. Why didn't you go first?"

Carlos ignored the whining and finished his brother's garbage armor. "It's a good thing we've got lots of supplies."

Once Mario's anti-sting armor was complete, Carlos started on himself.

Mario started pawing through the garbage pile again.

"What are you looking for?" Carlos asked.

"This." Mario held up a broken hand mirror. "Wow. I look even weirder than I thought." He stuck his arms out straight and started making groaning mummy noises.

"You look fine. Help me do my arms."

Mario's eyes danced. "Yeah. Together we will be the trash dead."

"Just don't waste the tape. We need every inch of it."

Concentrating, Mario's face scrunched. Finally finished, he grinned. "Now we look like mummy twins. There's still one trash bag left. Can I have a cape?"

"Sure," Carlos said. "And a helmet. You want the baseball cap or the cowboy hat?"

"You have to ask?" Mario grabbed the cap and slapped it on his head. "I'm the baseball star."

"Okay. Put on the gloves and sunglasses."

"Where's yours?" Mario asked.

"I don't need them," Carlos lied. They only had one pair. "I need to see clearly."

Carlos put the sunglasses on his brother and attached the yogurt cups over Mario's ears. Then he tied rags over both of their faces like banditos.

"Then take the gloves," Mario said, starting to pull them off.

Carlos shook his head. "Put them back on. I need my hands bare."

"Because?"

"Because I said so." Carlos turned on the radio and found a talk show.

"Hey," Mario complained. "I liked the music. The bees do, too."

Carlos turned up the volume and set the radio on the floor

by the pocket door. There still weren't any bees at the window. But they could hear the steady hum from the other room.

"Here's my plan," Carlos explained in detail. "I'll carry you piggyback. Once I open the front door we've got to move fast. And quiet. You ready?"

Mario nodded, his face hidden under all his gear.

"No improvising. Do exactly as I say. Got it?"

"Okay."

Carlos set the bear by the front door and slipped outside. He turned, motioning for Mario to climb on his back.

Mario wrapped his arms around Carlos's neck.

"You're choking me," Carlos whispered, trying to adjust Mario's weight. "Hang onto my shoulders. Not my neck."

Carlos reached for the toy bear and flipped its switch. The bear clanged its cymbals and sang over the talk show noise.

Gently, Carlos closed the Winnebago door, sealing the clanging bear and the blaring radio inside.

Gripping Mario's legs, he staggered toward the giant Saguaro cactus. Even though it lay only twenty feet ahead, it felt like a mile. The garbage armor crinkled with each step. Please. Don't let the bees realize we've escaped, he prayed.

A muffled, "Who let the dog out? Crash! Crash! Crash!" mocked every step.

The sun beat down like a furnace.

On Carlos's back, Mario squirmed. More crinkling. The plastic armor felt like a super sauna. Sweat pooled inside and Mario's hot breath tickled Carlos's neck.

The Saguaro loomed skyward. Up close it was huge. It had at least eight arms. Desert willow and bunchgrass surrounded its base. It was the perfect hiding place to catch his breath. If they could just reach it without alerting the bees—part one of his escape plan would be complete.

CHAPTER 15

Carlos helped Mario into a seating position on the ground, sheltered behind the huge cactus. The trick had worked, and the bees hadn't followed. The RV was less than twenty feet away. But the swarm wouldn't realize he was there if Mario stayed quiet.

Carlos leaned close and whispered the rest of the plan.

Mario's brows pinched in a frown. He looked confused. Then his eyes shot open wide like soccer balls. "No. I'm not staying here alone."

"You have to. It won't be long."

Mario tried to rise but Carlos pushed him down, leaned close, and whispered, "You can do this."

"But you're leaving me." Tears formed in Mario's eyes. "By myself."

"I'll be back. Soon. And this will all be over." Carlos squeezed Mario's shoulder. "Promise. Remember, you're like the invincible Spidey Man."

Mario nodded.

Carlos kept the Saguaro between himself and the RV and

crept away. The large cactus wasn't much of a shield, but better than nothing. He ran as fast as his short leg allowed—the duct-taped garbage bags crunching and crackling with every step.

Salty sweat stung his eyes. Swiping them only made things worse. He shot a frantic glance back over his shoulder as he retraced the short distance they'd crawled earlier under the inflatable pool.

Within seconds, he reached the garden shed. Nearby, the weed whacker lay abandoned near the clump of grass he'd torn from the ground. If only he hadn't yanked out that bunchgrass! But how was he supposed to know killer bees lived in his own yard? And how long did they have before the bees gave up on the Winnebago and came racing back here?

He was half-blind, roasting hot, and totally sweat-soaked. He knew the risk of a heat stroke and needed water but there wasn't time. Mario might get tired of waiting and do something stupid.

Carlos's guts twisted into a knot. Time to double hustle.

He grabbed his bike from its rack on the wall, rolled it out of the shed, and hopped on. This would be the race of his life. His well-trained muscles cranked the pedals up to speed. He flew over the dirt ground, sliding through uneven ruts, swerved around a prickly cactus, and skidded to a stop in front of Mario.

Mario clambered to his feet, looking spooked.

At the RV, the clanging toy bear had fallen silent, and a cloud of killer bees hovered around the broken window. A black mass hung along one outer wall, buzzing and swarming.

He was out of luck if he'd hoped they'd calmed down by now. They looked as angry as ever. Then again, killer bees stayed angry for hours—he'd even heard some stayed angry for days.

Roving sentry bees drifted in an ever-widening arc, on the alert for anything they decided was a threat within their hive's quarter-mile radius.

So far, they hadn't spotted the brothers.

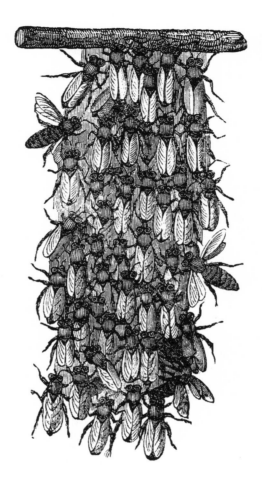

"Let's go," Carlos whispered.

Straddling the bike, Carlos half-lifted his brother onto the bike's trick bar.

Mario clung onto Carlos's back—with all his weight on his good leg.

"Hang on." Carlos pushed off, leaning sideways to counter-balance Mario's awkward sideways drag. He pumped hard a few times, trying to get moving. "Can you lean to the left a little?"

Mario shifted.

"Good. That's perfect."

Carlos panted through his mouth, slowly getting into gear. Riding with a passenger dangling a cast made it tricky. Especially cross-country over a dirt lawn studded with rocks. Right now, this was even slower than walking. But it was easier than carrying Mario on his back.

"Where are we going?" Mario gasped, sounding like he was in pain.

"Away. They'll lose interest pretty quick, as long as I keep riding."

"Wahoo!" Mario shouted. "Go faster, we're hardly moving."

"Shhhh! The bees." Carlos dug in, grunting as they bumped over clumps of dirt. "Look back. Are they following?"

"Oh no." Mario's voice was a hollow whisper. "They heard us. The swarm is coming."

Carlos went into panic mode.

"How close?" Carlos looked back and wished he hadn't.

The huge bee cloud detached from the RV wall and zoomed toward them.

Carlos pumped his legs. "As long as I don't stop, they won't catch us."

"How do you know that?" Mario said. "You said they can fly ten miles per hour."

"I pedaled faster than that in my last race," Carlos said. "I've got this."

"But you didn't have a passenger."

"Stop talking and hang on," Carlos said.

He left the lumpy yard and skidded onto Coyote Drive. The bike flew over a pothole, hit a rough patch of gravel, and sent both brothers flying. They hit the ground hard.

"Ow," Mario groaned as Carlos helped him to his feet.

They were out of time. The bees were closing in, and he needed a new plan, fast. They'd never get away down the dirt road. The riding was too rough with a broken-legged passenger clinging to Carlos's neck.

The Smiths' black iron gate was just across the gravel lane. The family was away but maybe they could get into the garage.

Carlos slung one arm around his brother and wheeled his bike up to the bars. The gate was electronically locked, but Carlos knew the code.

"They're getting closer," Mario said.

"Give me a sec."

Carlos punched 7- 4 - 6 -1 into the black box and waited for the gate to swing open. No response. Had he pushed a wrong number? Tried again. The gate didn't budge.

Had the Smiths changed their code when they left for vacation? They never had before.

"They're almost here," Mario yelled.

Carlos punched in the code a third time. Feeling stupid, this time he hit the star key.

The gate beeped, moving super slow—inch by inch.

"Get back on the bike!" Carlos told Mario. "Hurry!" The swarm was closing in. "Open, open, open!"

Carlos took off as soon as the space grew wide enough to fit through. The short driveway was paved—an easy ride if it wasn't uphill.

The bike careened upward.

"Faster. Faster," Mario cried.

Carlos pushed harder—they were nearly there.

The hill didn't slow the bees. It helped them. They shot up like helicopters in battle.

Carlos glanced at the garage with the sickening realization he'd never have time to open it, even if it was unlocked.

Glancing right, he saw the cool blue water of the Smiths' swimming pool. In the center floated a huge, inflated, pink flamingo—big enough to carry two adults.

Two recliner chairs blocked the way and forced him to slow.

The bees got closer.

Carlos slalomed between the chairs, past an outdoor table with an umbrella, and through scattered floaty noodles.

The swarm had almost caught up. The buzzing grew loud enough to vibrate the air.

"Hang on," Carlos shouted and felt a sting. He bit back a yelp.

"What are you doing?" Mario said. "Ouch! I'm stung."

"Take a big breath and hang on." Carlos aimed for the pink flamingo. Wrenching the handles, he punched down hard like in a takeoff at the track, and bunny-hopped into the air. The bike soared over the pool for two seconds before plunging into the water.

CHAPTER 16

T he chlorine water felt like a soothing blanket to Carlos's hot skin. Moving in slow-motion—every second stretched into a minute. The water pulled him to the bottom in a cool embrace. It felt so good. He could stay there forever.

Like he and Mario were fish. But by some miracle, he was still on his bike.

His eyes popped open. Where was Mario? He wasn't hanging on anymore. And Mario could hardly swim without a cast.

Still underwater, Carlos tried to kick away from the bike and couldn't. His foot was caught in the gear.

In total panic mode, he freaked. Pulled. Twisted. Tried to kick.

Bubbles escaped his mouth. Pinching his lips together, he tried to swallow the air in his mouth back into his lungs.

Looked up.

Mario floated under the big flamingo. Above the pool, bees skimmed its surface. Casting dark patches like storm clouds.

Shadows shifting. Growing darker. Thousands and thousands of angry bees.

Mario had been smart. His head was in the air cavity under the flamingo's body, and he held on with both hands.

Carlos's lungs felt like they there were about to burst. A trickle of tiny bubbles escaped his lips.

Bending double, he squinted to see what was caught in the gear. It looked like the garbage bag armor. Frantically, his fingers tore at the black plastic. It shredded but the silver duct tape didn't.

The strip wrapped around his ankle had caught in the gear. He tugged at it, using both hands. It held tight.

Another tiny escape of air. Fighting the urge to suck in a deep breath, his fingers felt for the end of the duct tape. Peeled its end back. Gripped it. Began unwinding the tape from his calf and ankle.

Suddenly his foot kicked free.

Pushing off the bottom, he shot upward, kicking, and arms flailing. His head jetted into the small air space next to his brother. Open-mouthed. Gasping.

"What were you doing?" Mario said. "It's been forever. A lot of help you were."

Carlos sucked in precious air and let Mario complain. His little brother didn't need to know he'd almost drowned.

"You did fine without me."

"Nice bunny hop." Mario grinned. "Do you realize we're in a flamingo butt?"

Carlos started breathing through his nose.

"Why did that news guy say that if bees attack, you're not supposed to jump into the water?"

"I don't know. You turned off the TV," Carlos said.

Mario winced. "It's hard to tread water in this stupid garbage armor."

"Don't complain. It worked." Carlos said.

"You took yours off."

"Only one leg. And I had to because—" Carlos stopped. Mario had had enough drama for one day. "You're right. We don't need it in the pool. Let's get to the shallow end. It'll be easier to take off if we can stand."

They floated the flamingo to the shallow end of the pool.

In short order, the pool was littered with the remains of their bee armor. Black plastic floated like dead crows while Duct tape shimmered like skinned eels.

A real mess. Carlos would clean it out before the Smiths arrived home next week. They were nice people. They'd understand.

"Can I take my cast off?" Mario said. "I don't think it fits anymore. It's heavy. And hurts my leg."

Carlos shook his head. "Mama will kill me."

"Please?" Mario looked like he was about to cry. "I'm not kidding. It hurts. A lot. Like when I broke it."

"Maybe it needs to be adjusted."

Carlos began to remove the cast and blanched. His brother's leg was purple and swollen. He quickly refastened it without taking it off. He didn't want to see any more.

"We're leaving it on."

CHAPTER 17

"It's stuffy," Mario said. "How long do we have to stay under here?"

Carlos didn't answer. The plan needed a little tweaking. Mario couldn't swim with his leg looking like that. "I'll snag some noodles."

"Sounds good. I'm hungry."

Carlos rolled his eyes. "A floaty noodle. I'll grab an extra one for you to chew on. Hot pink, green, or blue?"

"Ha ha," Mario said.

"I saw some poolside by the three-foot mark."

Carlos piloted the flamingo to where the floaties had been abandoned.

"Hold the flamingo. Don't move an inch. I'll be right back."

Carlos took a huge breath, dunked under the water, and headed for the black number three painted on the pool's side wall. A cloud of bees followed.

A lime-green noodle dangled over the edge. Keeping his head underwater, he reached into the air to grab the noodle.

Instantly his hand was covered in a live-bee glove—one full of stinging barbs.

He winced, tasting chorine.

Clutching the noodle, Carlos jerked his arm back into the pool.

The bees peeled off as they hit the water. Some escaped into the air. Some struggled on the surface. Others drowned.

Lungs bursting, he flipped off the side wall and swam to his brother.

Carlos popped up into the cramped airspace beneath the flamingo, huffing and puffing.

One look at his hand and he knew the bees had stung at least ten times. Felt like more. His fingers were already swelling into link sausages.

But getting the noodle was worth every sting. Mario needed the floating support. Who knew how long they'd be trapped under here? No one would be coming to save them now. No one even knew where they were.

"Ahh, what's that on your arm?" Mario said. The strain in his voice matched the fear on his face.

Carlos's skin rippled in terror as a soggy wet bee staggered toward his elbow. He slapped it hard. Lifeless, it dropped into the water. Lifting the edge of the flamingo, he flicked it under and away.

"Why did you do that?" Mario said. "It's dead."

"Dead, but its stinger can still sting."

Suddenly Carlos felt crawling sensations up his spine, in his hair, and even on his legs. It creeped him out. "See any bees on my back?"

Mario looked. "You're good. No bees."

Carlos sighed. "Okay. Ready to swim to the deep end?"

"Why?" Mario said. "I like it here. It's way better than under our plastic pool or the Winnebago. It's cool. And the bees can't swim." Pause. "Can they?"

"Don't think so."

Mario's face scrunched like he was trying to be brave and not cry. "I'm scared. Really scared. The bees are never giving up."

"We won't either," Carlos said. "Promise. Just one short lap and we win."

Mario didn't need to know that the air pocket would only last so long until the oxygen ran out. And if they let in air, it'd let in the bees, too.

They started moving. The bee cloud followed. To keep things light, Carlos said. "There are two unique things about this ool."

"Ool?" Mario's forehead wrinkled. "What's an ool?"

"It's what the Smiths call it."

"Why?"

"Because they don't allow any P in their ool." Carlos watched Mario's face morph from suspicion to surprise and into a lopsided grin.

"I get it," Mario laughed. "That's the first funny joke you've ever told."

"What do you mean? I tell jokes." Carlos breathed easier. Mario seemed less freaked out.

"Yeah, but they're not even close to funny." Mario chuckled.

"The second thing is that this is an indoor-outdoor pool."

Mario grinned again. "Is this another joke?"

"No. It's for real. I saw it the last time I was up here weeding. We're in the outside part of the pool. The indoor part is in the sunroom with the big windows."

"So, they have two pools."

"No. Just one. Half inside and half outside."

"Wow. That's fancy." Understanding lit his eyes. "How do we get in there?"

"We'll swim under the dividing wall and come up inside. There's a lounge area with a phone. We can call for help."

Mario chewed on his lower lip.

"Nothing can go wrong," Carlos said. "It's a short dive down and a short swim back up."

"I'll try," Mario said. "But my leg really hurts. I'm not sure I can do it."

"You don't have to. I'll tow you across the pool. You'll float." He grabbed the green floaty and realized his hand looked like a surgical glove blown up and ready to pop.

"Turn around," Carlos said, trying to hide his hand.

He wrapped the noodle under Mario's arms and tied it in a knot.

"Ready?" Carlos said.

"I guess so," Mario said.

Carlos started swimming, breathing hard in the enclosed space, with one hand on the flamingo and one hand on his brother. They passed the painted black three. Then the four. Then the five. Carlos spotted his bike twisted on the bottom—

his stomach wrenched. He couldn't afford to fix the Schwinn. Not this season. His BMX racing days were over.

But at least he and Mario were alive.

They reached the glass wall when he had a sudden, sickening thought. He'd once asked Mr. Smith how they kept thieves from swimming under the wall and entering the sunroom. That's when he'd learned about the underwater security gate.

What if it was locked?

CHAPTER 18

Carlos said a silent prayer. God, let it be open. Please? I'll never call Mario a pest again. Or even think it. And if I do, I'll never say it out loud.

"Why are we just sitting here?" Mario sounded nervous.

"I'm resting before I do a scouting dive," Carlos said. "You doing okay?"

"Yeah." Mario's tanned skin looked pale. Sickly.

"Great. I'll dive down to check the gate."

"There's a gate? What if it's closed?" Alarm crept into Mario's voice.

"If it is, I can open it," Carlos lied. "I'll be back. Practice holding your breath."

He sucked in a deep breath and plunged. The stainless-steel fence loomed ahead. Up close, it looked like a set of prison bars bolted to the submerged wall.

Was the gate locked?

He pulled and then pushed. The gate didn't budge. He tried jiggling it. Still closed. His lungs began to ache. He needed air and swam toward the flamingo, bursting into the now stale air pocket.

"Was it open?" Mario asked.

"I'm not sure. I ran out of air. I'll try again. But first I have to catch my breath."

"I practiced holding my breath," Mario said, "but it made me dizzy. I'm up to thirty seconds. Will that be long enough?"

"Try for forty. Fifty if you can."

Carlos pushed the Flamingo forward until it bumped into the glass wall. "Second time's the charm."

"Isn't it *third time's the charm*?" Mario said.

I hope not, thought Carlos and dived again. He reached the gate and felt for a handle or a release on the other side. Nothing.

He pushed and pulled again. Still nothing.

Desperate, he smacked the gate with both hands. It shifted to the right. Hope flared. Did it open like the pocket door in the RV by sliding sideways? Nearly out of air, he gave it one desperate shove. A two-foot space opened just big enough to swim through.

Yes!

Nearby, a snap dangled from a loop. He used it to clip the gate open and resurfaced.

"It's open. Ready?"

"I don't feel so good," Mario said. "I tried to hold my breath for as long as you were underwater. I couldn't."

"It won't take that long. You'll do fine."

Mario shook his head, "You go in and call for help. I'll wait here."

Carlos grabbed Mario's hand. It felt ice cold. Then he noticed his brother's eyes looked glassy. A thousand thoughts raced through his mind.

Was Mario allergic to bee stings? Was he having an allergic reaction? How many bee stings were too many? Or was it the stale air?

Carlos didn't know.

Maybe Mario had hurt his leg? It was swollen and bruised. Was it broken again?

Carlos didn't have the answers. All he knew is that his brother needed a doctor. Soon.

"Come on, let's get the noodle off," Carlos said. "You'll hang onto my back, and I'll swim you inside."

Mario didn't argue. Or complain. He just followed orders.

Once the noodle was removed, Carlos said, "On three, take a huge breath. Ready? One, Two. Three."

Carlos waited until he heard Mario gulp in air before diving deep into the pool. Swimming like a porpoise, he skimmed through the underwater door and popped up inside.

The pool steps were just a few feet away. He plunged up, dragging Mario to the surface. Mario gulped air and started sputtering.

It was muggy hot in the sunroom, and the smell of chlorine was strong. At least they could breathe.

"Hold on, buddy," Carlos said.

He settled his brother on the top step next to a handrail. White-faced, Mario slumped against it. His breathing grew ragged between moans.

"We're safe, you're going to be all right." Carlos ran for the phone, which sat on a small table near a gas BBQ.

Mario groaned and slid back into the pool.

"Hey!" Carlos shouted, raced to grab his brother's shirt, and pulled him onto the floor. "Wake up. Wake up, little brother. You can't quit on me. I can't do this alone. I need your help."

Mario whimpered. His eyelashes fluttered open. "You need me?"

Carlos nodded, his throat too tight to speak.

Mario's eyes closed.

Carlos's face went numb. "Mario."

After everything they'd gone through, why was this happening? Now? All they needed was another five minutes. And they'd be safe.

Carlos laid his ear on his brother's chest and listened for his brother's heartbeat.

CHAPTER 19

Carlos hated to leave Mario's side, but his brother's heartbeat was strong. He limp-ran toward the phone and a horrible sight slapped him in the face.

"What? No! That can't be."

One of the sunroom windows was open. So much for security—not that there was much to steal in here. He zipped into high gear and slammed it shut with his swollen hand.

Outside, the flamingo floated on the pool, surrounded by clouds of bees. Circling. Skimming the water. Hovering over the floating lounge.

Carlos's heart slowed. The bees were outside. Everything would be fine.

He snatched the phone just as a stab of pain pricked his ear.

Carlos yelped, dropping the phone. It clattered on the floor.

Something crawled across his cheek. He saw it from the corner of his eye and froze. A bee. It crept onto the bridge of his nose—right between his eyes. Vibrating before sinking its stinger into tender skin.

"Aaagh!'

He slipped and fell hard on the wet concrete floor. Looked up. Saw that his attacker wasn't alone. He counted twelve winged avengers, dive-bombing him in unison.

Carlos rolled onto his side and bumped into the BBQ. Frantic, he looked for something to cover his face and spotted a dishtowel on the bottom rack. He snagged it and slapped it over his mouth and nose.

That's when he saw the red canister strapped to the wall. A fire extinguisher. He crawled toward it.

The bees attacked from above, swarmed over his bare back, and stung. He ignored them and lifted the extinguisher from the wall with his good hand. He'd used one before and pulled the safety pin from its top. Squeezed the trigger.

White foam squirted from its nozzle.

Jumping to his feet, he held the extinguisher like he was Rambo. He aimed at the closest cluster of bees. The first foam blast took three down, covering them in sticky goo. They dropped. Wriggled helplessly.

He felt a sharp jab on his leg and sprayed it.

"Four down. Eight to go." Carlos's shout echoed in the room.

He jerked left. Jerked right. Slipping in the slimy foam. Aiming. Spraying. Managing to stay on his feet.

"Five down." Pause. "Six."

Another sting and he shot again, landing in an uncontrolled skid. "Seven. Eight. And nine down."

His short leg slipped and he landed flat on his back—the fire extinguisher clutched to his chest in a death grip. He aimed up and sprayed foam in a wild arc until the canister spewed only hissing air.

Three slimed bees dropped onto his torso. He flicked them to the floor and sat up, chest heaving. "Ten. Eleven. Twelve."

"Mario? Can you hear me?" Carlos grabbed the phone from the floor, punched in three numbers, and put it to his ear. "I'm calling 9-1-1."

The phone rang at the other end.

A calm dispatcher said, "911 emergency call center. What is your emergency?"

Carlos shouted into the phone. "My little brother and I were attacked by killer bees."

"Is there an adult I can talk to?"

"No. My brother needs a doctor," Carlos said. "Thousands of bees are outside."

"I see you're calling from 3197 Coyote Lane in Marana. Is that correct?"

"Yes."

"Emergency services will be dispatched immediately. Please stay on the line. I'll need more information."

Carlos took a deep breath and told her everything. Maybe not everything but enough. It felt like a miracle. Help was finally on its way.

"Carlos!" Mario called. "Come here."

"I've got to go," Carlos said.

"Don't hang up," the dispatcher said. "Stay on the line."

"I won't, but my brother needs me. He's only nine."

Mario had crawled to a lounge chair. "Can you help me up? The floor is hard."

"Sure." Carlos lifted him and propped him into a sitting position. "How does that feel?"

"Better. What happened to your face? It's all swollen. And so is your hand."

"While you were sleeping, I was in a bee battle." Carlos punched the air. "And I dominated."

"Looks like you lost. Does it hurt?"

"Not really," Carlos lied. Now that help was on the way, his arms, legs, and face felt like they had been used as a pincushion. "How about your leg?"

"I think I'll have to wear this cast for another six weeks."

Carlos raised his good hand. "High five?"

Mario slapped it. "Are the bees still out there?"

Together they turned and stared out the window. The bees had broken into smaller swarms. The largest swirled around the pink flamingo. Clouds of them skimmed the water. One mass hovered at the window. Others crawled on the glass.

"Do you think they'll ever leave?" Mario asked.

The faint screams of sirens grew louder until it sounded like they were next door.

The bees went crazy. Zipping left and right.

Emergency vehicles arrived in a burst of flashing red, blue, yellow, and orange lights. They raced through the open gate, up the short drive, and parked. Police Cars. Fire trucks. Sheriffs. Ambulances. Even a Channel 4 News van.

The bees gathered into what looked like a massive thundercloud and attacked.

The back doors of a big white truck were flung open. Men in hazmat suits swarmed into the backyard. They were armed with what looked like firehoses. Instead of water, they shot steady streams of foam exactly like he'd done with the fire extinguisher.

Carlos grinned at Mario. "I told you I had a great plan."

CHAPTER 20

3 DAYS LATER

Saturday morning, Carlos and Mario sat at the table. Bright sunlight streamed in through the kitchen window. They sipped hot chocolate while watching Mama finish cooking breakfast.

"You're lucky," Carlos said, fighting the urge to scratch. "You're not allergic to Benadryl. You look normal."

"You look normal, too," Mario said.

Carlos knew it was a lie. His face and right hand were still puffy and splotched. It was a small price. "Like the new cast?"

"Yeah. This one's cool because it's black."

"Who's hungry?" Mama said, setting a platter of steaming pancakes in the center of the table.

Carlos's stomach rumbled. Since the bee attack, he seemed to be starving all the time. Morning. Noon. Night. And in between.

Mario had already corralled the whipped cream, honey, and cinnamon sugar beside his plate. He leaned forward to stab a pancake with his fork.

"Hold on, mijo," Mama said, sitting down. "First, we say grace."

"Since when?" Mario complained.

"Since God saved you both from the bees."

"No, it was Carlos," Mario said. "He saved me from the bees."

"Mario," Mama's voice was stern. "Bow your head."

Mama said a short prayer of thanks for their family's safety and ended with an amen. "Mario. Don't take all the pancakes. Pass them to your brother."

Carlos loaded his plate and started eating.

"I love Saturdays," Mario said, talking with his mouth full. "Because we get cinnamon pancakes. And there's no school."

"Speaking of school," Mama said. "You both need to finish your assignments from the days you missed."

"That's not fair. Carlos and I are heroes. We shouldn't have to do make-up work."

Carlos grinned. Mario was back to his usual self.

Mama rolled her eyes. "Do you want to repeat the fourth grade?"

Mario frowned. "Can we talk about something else? Hey, I've got a new joke. What kind of bees can fly in the rain?" Pause. "The ones wearing yellow jackets." He giggled.

Carlos groaned. "I've heard enough bee jokes. Save them for your friends."

"Are you still afraid of bees?"

"I probably should be, but not really. At least not like before. I'm just tired of bee jokes."

"But I have to practice my timing."

The landline rang. Carlos hopped up. "I'll get it." He answered, listened, frowned, and covered the speaker. "Mama, It's your boss."

Mama took the phone and stepped away into the pantry.

Why did the boss always call Mama in on Saturdays? She deserved the day off. They could call someone else. He got that they needed the money and that sometimes doing the right thing wasn't fun. But every Saturday?

He'd have to spend the day with Mario. And today was race day—he'd planned to go and watch his team win.

Polishing off his last bite, he licked the honey from his lips.

Defeating the killer bees was a bittersweet victory. They'd ruined everything. His precious bike. The opportunity to impress the man from Wolf Racing. The chance of the sponsorship. The chance to help Mama with the bills.

It was all a lost dream.

Mario hobbled into the living room. The television came on.

Carlos set the dirty dishes in the dishwasher and joined his brother.

The TV was tuned to News 4 Tucson. UPDATE MARANA BEE ATTACK flashed across the screen in a red banner.

Mario turned up the volume.

"We have an update on the condition of the two boys attacked by a massive swarm of African Killer bees in Marana," the news anchor said.

"We're on TV again," shouted Mario.

Carlos and Mario's school pictures appeared on the screen. Then it cut to a video of Mario being wheeled on a gurney with Carlos, face swollen and limping at his side.

"The Mendoza brothers were released from the hospital yesterday. The heroic efforts of—."

"Haven't you watched that enough?" Mama said, shutting it off. "You've seen it a dozen times already." She shook the car keys. "Let's go if you want to make the first race."

"You're not going to work?" Carlos said.

"No. I told Mr. Baker I had a previous commitment. He'd have to find someone else to cover the shift."

"Thanks, Mama," Carlos said and gave her a hug.

They loaded into the car. Mario with his crutches, Carlos

with a hat to hide his lumpy head. And Mama with a big secret smile. Twenty minutes later, they arrived at the BMX Ranch.

The races wouldn't start for another half hour. Still, the parking lot was jammed. They had to park in the back next to a big white travel van.

Luis slid to a stop by the car, all tricked out in his racing gear. "How's the hero? Everyone is talking about it at school."

"I'm okay." Carlos pulled his hat lower.

Mario got out and high-fived Luis.

"How many stings, little man?" Luis asked.

"Eighteen," Mario said. "Carlos got stung thirty-five times. The doctor said it's lucky he isn't allergic to bees."

Luis winced. "I can't imagine—"

"You don't want to," Carlos said with a grin.

"Come on. Coach wants to see you before the races start. He's over there by the bleachers." Luis looked at Mario and Mama. "You guys can come, too, and grab a seat."

Coach and the whole team were waiting. Plus, a bunch of strangers and Channel 4 News. Huge grins were plastered on everyone's faces. They clapped and cheered when they spotted Carlos. His face grew warm. He wasn't used to being the center of attention. Not like this. And definitely not with a puffy face.

Coach motioned for Carlos to join him on the track. He followed awkwardly until he stood alone by Coach's side. Everyone was watching. What was going on?

The crowd fell silent.

Coach put a hand on Carlos's shoulder and smiled. Then, he raised a microphone and said, "The team heard your bike didn't survive the killer bee attack, so—"

Sweat trickled down Carlos's neck. His heart pounded. Time seemed to slow. Standing in front of this many people staring at him, even if some were his friends, was almost as frightening as being chased by the killer bees.

Coach continued. "The team, community members, the BMX

Ranch, Channel 4 News, and Wolf Racing joined together to present you with a new bike."

Carlos stared wide-eyed at Coach.

The crowd stomped their feet and started chanting, "Bee Racer."

"Look," Coach said and pointed.

Luis pushed the latest GT Speed series BMX onto the track. It had sleek lines and was painted a gun-metal green, Carlos's favorite color.

He could hardly believe this awesome bike was his. The team and all these people had actually pitched in to get this for him. Was this for real?

A huge grin split his face. "Wow," was all he could say.

That seemed enough, though, for the crowd broke into fresh cheers.

"Bee racer!" they chanted. "Bee Racer, Bee Racer!"

Luis slapped his shoulder. "You earned it."

"Thanks," Carlos said hoarsely, his gaze glued to the bike. It was perfect.

He couldn't wait to race it. But that would be after the pedal was altered to fit his shorter leg. He couldn't compete riding off balance. Then Carlos's jaw dropped. The pedal had already been modified.

"If you can tear your eyes off your new bike," Coach said. "Karl Ericksen from Wolf Racing has an additional presentation to make."

Coach handed the microphone to a tall, tanned man dressed in Wolf Racing gear. The man shook Carlos's hand like Carlos was an adult.

"So, you are the bike hero I've heard so much about," Mr. Ericksen said, handing him a Wolf Racing duffle bag. "Wolf Racing would like to recognize your bravery and present you with comfortable gear used by our BMX star racers."

The people stood, cheered, clapped, and stomped their feet.

Coach took back the mic and pointed toward Carlos.

Carlos leaned over and shouted out, "Thank you. Thank you so much."

"First race starts in fifteen minutes," Coach announced to the crowd. "Which gives you all time to visit the Snack Shak. All proceeds from today will go to the winning team."

"I'm looking forward to seeing you race today," Mr. Ericksen said. "Good luck."

Carlos wheeled the bike over to show Mama and Mario.

Mama was grinning.

"Mom, you knew?" Carlos said.

She nodded and hugged him. "You better get changed. Mr. Ericksen called me for your sizes. He said there's everything you'll need in the bag."

Mario was hopping up and down. "I bet it's a bunch of cool

stuff. You're going to outride everyone. You can't lose. You're going to win."

Carlos laughed. "I don't know about that. What I *do* know is that I outrode the bees, we're safe, and that's what really counts." He gently knuckle-rubbed Mario's head. "Together, we escaped the killer bee attack!"

THE END

Turn the page for amazing facts about bees and more!

10 Fast Facts About Killer Bees

1. Africanized honeybees look just like common European honeybees.
2. The average honeybee calms down in a few minutes. Africanized killer bees can hold a grudge and stay aggressive for hours. Also, killer bees respond to a threat in less than 5 seconds, while European honeybees take up to 30 seconds to react.
3. They nest in cavities—holes in the ground, tree trunks, discarded tires, or any crevice, like attic spaces.
4. A small Africanized beehive can have 40,000 bees.
5. Africanized bees can continuously sting their target over and over.
6. They're attracted to perfume or strong-smelling sunscreen.
7. They can fly 10 to 15 miles per hour. Be prepared to run up to the length of two football fields.
8. Bees attack where carbon dioxide is expelled. For example, your breath. Your face will be the first area to be stung.
9. If you jump into a pool, the bees will wait until you surface to attack.
10. If you are swarmed by Africanized bees, you have a 25% percent chance of survival.

KILLER BEE QUOTES

"The minute I got out of the car, I started getting attacked… All of a sudden it [the swarm] just attacked me on my face. I thought I hit a tree."
   - Steve Gluskin told 12 News

"People mustn't bother a bee . . . [here in Arizona] They have a little bit of African in them and a little bit of European, so you never know how to mean they could be."
   - Elliot Ginn, Beekeeper

"There is no way to tell the difference between bees, so all bees have to be handled with caution."
   - Dan Armijo, Exterminator

"As soon as the bees start stinging it's time to leave, and it's time to leave fast. And don't stop."
   - Scott the Bee Man

"I've been with the fire department for 18 years now and responded to several bee incidents. But never to this magnitude ... The bees were very aggressive."

- Lisa Derderian, Pasadena Fire Department Public Information Officer, February 22, 2020

"They'll continue to go after you."

- Jeff Pettis, United States Department of Agriculture's Bee Research Lab

"There were up to 500 stingers in her. She swelled up and has been intubated ever since [ten days later]."

- Jerry Nassif, whose wife was stung by hundreds of Africanized bees

"Several people were injured and one person passed away due to their injuries."

- Marana police officer, July 30, 2021

DID YOU KNOW?

READ ON FOR MORE FASCINATING FACTS ABOUT BEES

BEES ARE IMPORTANT!

Bees give us more than honey. In fact, most bees don't make honey. The ones that don't are called solitary bees. There are about 20,000 different types of bees. Wow!

One-third of the U.S. food production depends on them. They pollinate flowers that turn into fruit, vegetables, plants, and trees.

How? Bees carry pollen on their bodies and legs from one flower to another. Solitary bees are fantastic pollinators because they spill more pollen than they bring back to their hives. One solitary Red Mason bee spreads more pollen than 120 worker honeybees.

Why is spreading pollen important?

The pollen fertilizes plants, which allows them to grow fruits and vegetables. Can you imagine a world without apples, oranges, or carrots?

SOLITARY BEES

Solitary bees get their name because they don't hang out in big hives with lots of other bees. Each female is a Queen bee and worker bee rolled into one. First, she builds a tube nest. Then she sets a ball of pollen mixed with nectar at the end of the tube and lays an egg on it. Next, she builds a wall to separate this egg from the next one. She repeats the process until the tube is filled.

What's cool is that she chooses whether to lay male or female eggs.

Female eggs are always laid first and males second.

Why?

Because male bees hatch quicker than females.

A solitary bee lives for between one and three years and lays around twenty to thirty eggs in her short lifetime.

HONEYBEES

Honeybees live in colonies. Each hive has one queen bee, many female worker bees, and male drones. They all have jobs.

The queen bee lays the eggs—over 1,500 a day! The worker bees clean the hive, collect pollen and nectar, and care for the offspring. The drone's only job is to mate with the queen.

Only female bees can sting. The venom is stored in a sac attached to its stinger. Most bees can only sting once.

Another three interesting facts: They can see all colors except red. They can see far. And they can smell even farther.

HOW AFRICANIZED BEES ARE LIKE THEIR HONEYBEE COUSINS

Africanized bees look similar, but the honeybee is slightly larger. It takes a bee expert to see the difference.

They both produce honey.

They both respond to what they feel are threats in the same way: by stinging intruders.

Both types of stings deliver the same dose of venom.

Their colonies are made up of a queen bee, male drones, and female worker bees.

Their queen bees can lay over 1,500 eggs per day.

HOW AFRICANIZED BEES ARE *DIFFERENT* THAN THEIR HONEYBEE COUSINS

A European bee colony produces five times more honey than an Africanized bee colony.

Because Africanized bees are quicker to respond and sting without limits, they are more dangerous.

They attack in greater numbers and pursue their victims for greater distances. Plus, the killer bee colony can remain agitated longer.

Killer bees react to noises or vibrations even when there is no threat. There is no retreat. They will chase a person for up to a quarter of a mile.

Killer bees have a shorter development time frame and quickly grow into 40,000 bees.

There is a 75% chance of being in a deadly attack if you are in the path of a killer bee swarm.

HOW DID AFRICANIZED KILLER BEES END UP IN THE UNITED STATES?

Over seventy years ago, a scientist in Brazil was trying to produce a better honeybee. Unfortunately, an experimental queen bee escaped and migrated north. It took forty years for them to arrive in the United States. Jesus Lopez was the first American to be stung. He survived, but two years later, Lino Lopez died from a bee attack.

The killer bees like warmer climates and are primarily found in the southern States. (Texas, Arizona, California, Nevada, New Mexico, Oklahoma, Louisiana, Arkansas, and Florida)

TAKE HEART

Swarming bee attacks do happen, but you're more likely to be struck by lightning than to be killed in a bee attack.

SAFETY TIPS

If you live in an area where there are killer bees . . .BEE SMART!

- If you see a swarm, get inside your house or car. Close the doors and windows.
- Don't play dead.
- Don't scream or wave your arms.
- Don't swat at the bees.
- If you're outside, run as fast as you can in a straight line. Bees can chase you up to 200 hundred yards.
- Protect your face. Pull your shirt over your head to prevent stings to your eyes, nose, or mouth.
- Don't jump into a pool or a lake. The bees will wait for you to come up for air and attack.
- Be careful while using loud lawn equipment.
- Never attempt to remove a hive on your own. Leave it to the experts.

More Mario Bee Jokes

When do bees get married?
  When they find their honey!

Why was the bee was fired from the barber shop?
  Because he could only give buzz-cuts.

What's a happy bumblebee's blood type?
  Bee positive!

What kind of bee is hard to understand?
  A mumble-bee!

What did one bee say to the other when they landed on the same flower?
  Buzz off!

What do you get when you cross a doorbell and a bee?
  A hum-dinger.

What's a bee's favorite sport?
  Rug-bee.

What is the last thing to go through a bee's mind when it hits a windshield?
  I'll bee seeing you.

What do you call a bee that's been put under a spell?
  Bee-witched!

KILLER BEE RESOURCES

Learn even more with these useful resources!

National Geographic video:
https://www.youtube.com/watch?v=d-7kKqgPEGs

**Arizona Department of Transportation
Safety Briefing:**
https://azdot.gov/business/programs-and-partnerships/
adopt-highway/safety-requirements/safety-briefing

BEE CULTURE
The Magazine of American Bee Keeping
https://www.beeculture

United States Department of Agriculture (USDA)
Invasive Species Information
Africanized Honeybee
https://www.invasivespeciesinfo.gov/terrestrial/
invertebrates/africanized-honeybee

THE I ESCAPED SERIES

I Escaped North Korea!

I Escaped The California Camp Fire

I Escaped The World's Deadliest Shark Attack

I Escaped Amazon River Pirates

I Escaped The Donner Party

I Escaped The Salem Witch Trials

I Escaped Pirates In The Caribbean

I Escaped The Tower of London

I Escaped Egypt's Deadliest Train Disaster

I Escaped The Haunted Winchester House

I Escaped The Gold Rush Fever

I Escaped The Prison Island

I Escaped The Grizzly Maze

I Escaped The Killer Bees

More great adventures coming soon!

JOIN THE I ESCAPED CLUB

Get a free pack of mazes and word finds to print and play!

https://www.subscribepage.com/escapedclub

Made in the USA
Middletown, DE
28 January 2024

48668868R00068